Greenbeck Village GPs

Love is in the air at Greenbeck Surgery!

It's more than just the patients who find healing at Greenbeck Surgery—for the tight-knit group of medics who work there, the surgery is the perfect prescription for second chances and the possibility of finding love! For busy GP and single mom Stacey Emery, a night of passion with her widowed colleague GP Daniel Prior leads to a pregnancy surprise. And for wary nurse Hannah Gladstone, an impulsive decision to fake date her new boss, GP Zach Fletcher, turns into a romance neither of them expects!

Get cozy with a cup of tea for these heartfelt romances by Louisa Heaton.

Enjoy

Stacey and Daniel's story
The Brooding Doc and the Single Mom

and

Hannah and Zach's story
Second Chance for the Village Nurse

Both available now!

Dear Reader,

In this book, I wanted to take a look at the effects of loneliness. Being alone can be an awful thing to have to deal with, and so for this book, in which we get to explore the love story between Dr. Zachary Fletcher and advanced nurse practitioner Hannah Gladstone, I wanted to show what being lonely can do to people.

My solution? Dogs!

Not everyone can have a dog, though, and so Hannah sets up a walking group for lonely people to get together and walk some dogs from a local rescue center. It's good for the dogs, it's great for the people, and the lonely residents who reside in Greenbeck get companionship and the opportunity to make new friends.

One particular dog in this story, Rebel, provides a moment that was a joy to write. I'll let you work out which one!

I hope that you enjoy your brief stay in Greenbeck and also hope that one day you will return. Maybe over and over again.

Happy reading!

Love,

Louisa x

SECOND CHANCE FOR THE VILLAGE NURSE

———

LOUISA HEATON

HARLEQUIN
MEDICAL
ROMANCE

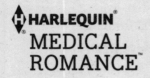

HARLEQUIN®
MEDICAL ROMANCE™

Recycling programs for this product may not exist in your area.

ISBN-13: 978-1-335-73789-2

Second Chance for the Village Nurse

Copyright © 2023 by Louisa Heaton

Harlequin Enterprises ULC
22 Adelaide St. West, 41st Floor
Toronto, Ontario M5H 4E3, Canada
www.Harlequin.com

Printed in U.S.A.

Louisa Heaton lives on Hayling Island, Hampshire, with her husband, four children and a small zoo. She has worked in various roles in the health industry—most recently four years as a community first responder, answering 999 calls. When not writing, Louisa enjoys other creative pursuits, including reading, quilting and patchwork—usually instead of the things she *ought* to be doing!

Books by Louisa Heaton

Harlequin Medical Romance

Greenbeck Village GPs

The Brooding Doc and the Single Mom

Reunited at St. Barnabas's Hospital

Twins for the Neurosurgeon

Their Unexpected Babies
The Prince's Cinderella Doc
Pregnant by the Single Dad Doc
Healed by His Secret Baby
The Icelandic Doc's Baby Surprise
Risking Her Heart on the Trauma Doc
A Baby to Rescue Their Hearts
A GP Worth Staying For
Their Marriage Meant To Be
Their Marriage Worth Fighting For
A Date with Her Best Friend
Miracle Twins for the Midwife

Visit the Author Profile page at Harlequin.com.

To all my friends at LWS x

CHAPTER ONE

Three months ago

'Wow. You can really be wrong about some people, huh?' Dr Zachary Fletcher said after the interviewee had left the room. He stood, stretched out his back muscles and let out a sigh. 'Tea?' he asked Lucy, the practice manager.

It had been a long, exhausting day, interviewing potential candidates not only for the new GP spot they were opening up, but also to replace their advanced nurse practitioner, who had left after moving closer to family.

Both he and Lucy had agreed on the new GP—Dr Stacey Emery, whom they had interviewed via video call, was the perfect candidate for their team. But they were struggling with finding the right nurse practitioner.

Their surgery was a small practice at the heart of the Greenbeck community, and Zach had worked hard to choose staff who fitted in with the type of practice he was trying to create. Warm, approachable, team players... He'd seen some great nurse practitioners today. But were any of them the right fit for Greenbeck?

The last one had had a great CV, that was for sure, but her personality wasn't what he was looking for. In the interview she'd come across as a little abrupt, a little sharp, and had responded to their questions in a prickly manner—almost as if she'd thought they were being nosy. But a job interview demanded that the employer ask questions. It wasn't just about qualifications. It was about finding the right person.

'It's a shame we can't make it Irish tea. But plain old boring tea will have to recharge us so we can get through this last one.' Lucy picked up the application form with a heavy sigh. 'Hannah Gladstone. Happy to relocate if offered the job.'

Zach switched on the kettle. 'Where does she live now?'

Lucy perused Hannah's letter of application. 'Epsom.'

'Okay. Well, let's hope she's amazing— because we've run out of applicants.'

He made the tea, and offered Lucy biscuits from the tin, before he sat down and sipped at his own drink and scanned the application. It all looked good, but so had the last one, so...

'Ready?' he asked.

Lucy smiled. 'As I'll ever be.'
'Okay. Let's go.'

It was a nice waiting room. Modern. Brightly decorated. In one corner there was a large bookcase filled with children's books that had a sign above it informing parents that children could borrow books and take them home.

Like a kids' library, Hannah thought, smiling.

There were the usual noticeboards, filled with posters informing patients of both sexes of the value of checking themselves for lumps and/or anything different from usual. And a sign stating that breastfeeding was welcome in the waiting area or, if the mother preferred, a private room could be supplied, which was nice. Behind the reception desk were photographs of the surgery during its rebuild—doctors and nurses, office staff and receptionists. Everyone was smiling.

Would her face end up on the wall? Hannah wondered. She doubted it. Clearly she was the last interview of the day. The interviewers would be tired, or just ready to get home. They would have heard all the clever answers to their questions already.

What are your strengths?
What are your weaknesses?

Why should we hire you and not one of the other candidates for the job?

The reception team were less busy now than they had been when she'd first arrived. Appointments were being wrapped up. There was only Hannah and a young mother still waiting. The mum was on her phone while her infant lay back in her buggy, mouthing a rusk. The young woman looked up and over at Hannah.

She smiled politely, her stomach churning with nerves. She wasn't good at job interviews. Not any more. They'd never used to bother her, but since the accident and everything that had happened with Edward, her ex-fiancé, her self-confidence had taken a bit of a dive. To sit in front of people assessing her, judging her, reminded her too much of the past. Put under pressure, she stuttered, or said the wrong thing as she waited for the other person to realise that she wasn't worth their trouble. Or worse…they pitied her.

But I need this job! I need to get away from where I am.

There was a caught thread puckering her dark trousers, midway down her right thigh. She'd never noticed it before. Frowning, she tried to smooth it out, but her nail caught on it and pulled it more instead. It looked awful, suddenly. Exposing a small hole the size of a pea that revealed her thigh. She looked as if she couldn't afford a decent pair of trousers, and she hated to think that the interviewers' eyes would be drawn there.

'Shannon Glossop?'

The young mum got up and wheeled her baby down the corridor towards a woman in uniform. A nurse? An HCA? She couldn't tell.

Now Hannah was alone in the waiting room, feeling sweat forming in her armpits and running down her back. Her mouth was dry. Was there a water fountain? She looked about her and saw one in the far corner. She put her bag down and went over to pour herself a drink of cold water.

She was just about to take a sip when a deep, slightly accented voice said, 'Miss Gladstone?' and she jumped, spilling the water down her white silk top.

Hannah looked down at herself in dismay.

Damp top. Hole in trousers. Perfect.

'Are you all right?'

She turned, cheeks flushing wildly, knowing she must look a mess, to see a man standing before her.

Tall. Dark-hair, slightly tousled. Cheeky blue eyes and a great smile. He was looking at her strangely.

Probably he's hoping that I'm not his interviewee!

Hannah brushed her top down, trying to wipe off the excess water. 'Y-yes. I'm f-fine. I'm sorry I spilt all that…maybe if there's a mop I could…? Sorry. Hannah Gladstone.'

She held out her hand for him to shake, realised the cup was still in it and hurriedly swapped it over, spilling more, forcing a smile, and hoping he couldn't feel her trembling as he shook her hand.

He was simply the most remarkable-looking man she'd ever seen in her life. Was he for real? The temptation to pinch him and check that he wasn't wearing some sort of mask was overwhelming.

'Don't worry about that. We'll get it sorted. Put up a sign…'

He smiled at her, which she almost didn't notice, so lost was she in listening to his soft Scottish burr. Which part of Scotland was he from? Glasgow? Edinburgh? She suddenly wished she knew everything there was to know about Scotland, just so she could talk to him about it and listen to him speak. There was something so mesmerising about the lilt and flow of his speech she almost forgot what she was there for.

Job interview. Come on, now. Snap to it!

'Oh, r-right. Thank you. If you're sure?'

He nodded and smiled again. His smile revealed a row of lovely white teeth and his eyes gleamed with amusement.

It was something she was familiar with, having received a fair amount of amused looks over the last year or so. She'd become a figure of ridicule back home. At least that was how it felt, and although she knew she shouldn't care so much about what others thought of her she couldn't help it. She was too sensitive.

'We're just in here.'

He stood back and indicated that she should go into the room ahead of him. Inside, a woman sat behind a desk with a pile of papers, upon which sat Hannah's application. Next to that was a mug of tea and a plate of fruit shortcake biscuits.

The woman stood. 'Miss Gladstone?' She smiled.

'Hannah. Yes.' She shook the woman's hand.

'Please take a seat. My name is Lucy Dent and I'm the practice manager here in Greenbeck, and this is Dr Zachary Fletcher, the senior partner.'

Zachary... Zach... It suited him, she thought, turning and smiling even harder as he closed the door behind her, slipped past, and indicated that she should sit before he settled into his chair opposite her.

'I hope you found us all right?' asked Dr Fletcher.

'Eventually! I followed your instructions, but still somehow got lost.' She laughed, assuming they'd laugh with her, but then realised she was on a job interview and needed to seem competent. 'I mean, I know how to follow directions, of course... I'm just not very... I struggle with...' She laughed nervously. 'I'm just not that good with maps.' She blushed madly and leaned in. 'Good thing I'm not a pirate! Not that pirates are...'

She bit her lip. Knew she was babbling. She glanced at Zach and saw that he was staring at her with a confused smile. She sucked in a breath. Gathered herself.

Stop panicking.

'I got here just fine—thank you.'

'I'm glad to hear it.'

He glanced at Lucy and they shared a look.

Hannah felt her heart drop like a stone.

I'm ruining it!

'So, why don't you tell us about yourself, Miss Gladstone?' suggested the practice manager.

She nodded. She could do that, right?

'Erm...well... I'm Hannah, and I've been working as an advanced nurse practitioner for about ten years now. I've been at the same GP practice all that time—it was my first job—and now I'm looking for a change.'

'And that's full-time?' asked Dr Fletcher, looking down at her application form.

'Yes. Full-time. Well, mostly... I...er...had an accident and was off work for a while, and when I came back I had a phased return, but then I went back to full-time.'

He nodded. 'I'm sorry to hear that. How long ago was that?'

'Two years ago.'

'You're fit and well now?'

'Absolutely! One hundred percent. Tip-top.'

Why the hell did I say tip-top? When have I ever, in my entire life, said tip-top?

Lucy smiled at her. 'What would you consider to be your strengths?'

'Oh, gosh... Well, not job interviews, that's for sure!'

She laughed, self-deprecatingly, thinking they'd join in—only they didn't. They looked at her with amusement, but didn't laugh.

This is not going well.

'I'm a good nurse practitioner. I am. It may not seem like it. I don't think I'm giving you the best impression. But that's my weakness, you see? I babble when I'm nervous, or I go silent completely—which, looking at you now, I'm guessing you wish was the case today. But... I make a mean cup of tea and I'm kind and considerate. I *love* talking to my patients and building a trusting relationship with them and...'

Suddenly her brain went astoundingly blank and her mouth gaped open as she fought desperately for something positive to say that would make them change their minds.

'I'm...er...'

She closed her mouth, looking down. She saw the hole in her trousers and thought about how badly this was going. Felt herself deflate. Felt all the fight go out of her.

'I'm a good person...' It was all she could manage.

The rest of the interview didn't go any better.

With her fight gone, and her sense of optimism about getting this job disappearing faster than a bullet from a gun, Hannah felt she waffled her way through all their questions. Never saying anything persuasive and certainly not saying anything that would make these two think they ought to employ her.

'Do you have any questions you'd like to ask us?' said Lucy at the end.

And even though she'd practised many of them in the car, such as, *Would I get the opportunity to run training courses regularly to maintain* she figured she'd failed at this interview anyway, so what did it matter?

'When do I start?' she said, and laughed, joking.

Her smile died on her face when she saw the two of them look at each other once again, before looking back at her quizzically.

'Look, I would like to thank you for seeing me. I appreciate your time. But I could have done much better.'

She stood and shook their hands. Then she took one last final look at Dr Zachary Fletcher, just so she could imprint his face on her memory and go home and tell her best friend Melody all about him. Not that she'd be likely to forget his face…it was just so attractive. But it would have been nice to think she could look at it for as long as she wanted if she got this post.

'You're welcome. We'll be in touch,' he said, and that Scottish burr soothed her jangling nerves.

She headed back out into Reception, thanked the reception staff, and then put her bag on a waiting room chair so she could search for her car keys. Once she'd found them she headed outside, and walked straight into the young mother she'd seen earlier, colliding with her.

'My baby! She's choking!'

What?

Hannah dropped her bag and rushed over to the mother's car—and, yes, the young mum was right. Her baby was strapped into her car seat and appeared to be choking on something.

She turned and said urgently, 'Go into the surgery—get more help!'

She wrestled with the safety lock, unfastening it and pulling the baby free. The obstruction couldn't be seen, and she didn't dare risk putting her finger in to hook the obstruction in case she forced it down further. She supported the infant on the length of her arm, face down, and began to deliver some blows to her back, between the baby's shoulder blades.

The baby still coughed and spluttered, and just when Hannah thought the child was in danger of passing out, the obstruction flew out of the baby's mouth and landed on the car park concrete. Half a grape.

The young mum came running out of the surgery, followed by Dr Fletcher and Lucy and another male—a doctor, by the looks of it, armed with a go bag. Their faces relaxed when they heard the baby burst into tears after such a shocking and scary experience.

'She's okay now. She's okay,' Hannah said, handing the upset baby back to her mum. 'But maybe you ought to get one of the doctors to give her the once-over, just to be sure.'

The young mum nodded and walked over to

the other medic, another handsome young man, with a fashionable short trimmed beard.

They headed back into the surgery and Dr Fletcher watched them go, then turned back to appraise her and smiled. 'Well done. You just saved that baby's life.'

'Oh, anyone would have done the same.'

'A lot of people would have panicked, seeing a baby choking like that. You showed some skills, and best of all you remained calm and did what needed to be done.' He seemed to think about something, then grinned. 'How quickly can you give notice?'

'I'm sorry?' She stared at him, not sure she was understanding. He had to be joking, right?

'Would you like the job?'

When he smiled, his whole face lit up…eyes sparkling.

'This one? Here?' She pointed at the surgery, trying to make sure she understood correctly.

'That would be the one I am referring to, yes.'

'You're sure?'

'One hundred percent.'

She laughed. This was crazy! *Really?* Was he just offering her the job out of sympathy?

'But I did awfully in the interview!'

'You were nervous.' He shrugged.

'I was terrible!'

'No.' He shook his head, and as he turned to go he laughed and said, 'You were *tip-top*.'

CHAPTER TWO

Present day

ZACH HAD WORKED extremely hard to build this team, this family feel at the Greenbeck surgery. He'd not wanted to start a practice where a bunch of people just came into work each day, did their hours and then clocked off. He'd wanted to create a place of work where people looked forward to coming in every day. Where the people he employed were more than team players. Where they were like family—only without all the arguments or secrets or jealousies.

Hannah had been a strange, energetic, babbling, nervous bundle of energy at her interview, but she had made him smile in a way he hadn't smiled for a while. He'd known she was perfectly qualified and had the experience he was looking for just from seeing her application form. What he'd wanted to judge was her character, and whether she would fit into Greenbeck with them all.

Her job interview had been…well, a *disaster*. He'd seen in her eyes the moment she'd thought she'd lost them, and even though he'd kept asking her questions to show her that he was still interested, that she still had time to pull things back, he'd realised her confidence had taken one hell of a knock. Something had knocked the stuffing out of this beautiful young woman, and he'd found himself wanting to help her.

But the interview had ended so badly he'd begun to think that maybe he was wrong. Maybe she'd be perfect in a year or two, when she had built up more confidence in herself? And then she'd astounded him when she'd saved that baby's life in the car park on her way out. It had been in that moment, when Hannah had passed the baby back to the mother, that he'd seen in her eyes the confidence she had in her skills and her ability to know what the right thing to do was.

She'd known how to handle the panicking mother, she'd managed to send for help, and afterwards she hadn't seemed to want any accolades for what she had done. She had been humble. As if it was an everyday occurrence. And he'd known there and then that she was the nurse he'd been looking for.

Now he was waiting for her and the new

doctor, Dr Stacey Emery, to arrive for their first day. They both had appointments today, but their time allotment for each patient had been doubled from ten minutes to twenty, to give them time to get used to being somewhere new. If there was anything they weren't sure of, it would give them extra time—to find necessary items or go and ask for advice—without the appointments falling behind and creating long waits for the patients who were still in the waiting room.

For some reason he felt nervous, but he told himself it was because he wanted today to go well. And that worked until he saw new advanced nurse practitioner Hannah Gladstone walk into the main reception area, holding a plastic tub filled with what looked like cookies, and smile at everyone. Just watching her introduce herself to everyone made his mouth go dry and his heart pound hard in his chest as she came closer and closer to him.

Just excited to actually see her here. That's all. Building the work family. Glad my instincts were right.

He noticed an almost imperceptible limp. Her left leg. From the accident she'd mentioned? She seemed to be in a little discomfort but hid it well.

'Good morning, Dr Fletcher.' She stood before him, her eyes twinkling with excitement and nerves. 'Cookie?'

He held up his hand to refuse. He was trying to watch what he ate, and it was too early for him to have sugar. 'Zach, please. All moved in okay?'

'Yes! Thank you. It's a little weird, waking up to birdsong and cows mooing outside my window, rather than car alarms blaring or sirens, but I'm sure I'll get used to it.'

'Mrs Micklethwaite will take good care of you.'

'Well, I was just lucky she had a room that I can lodge in. Trying to find a place in Greenbeck is extremely difficult.'

He nodded, agreeing. Their other new member of staff, Dr Emery, was going to lodge in Dr Daniel Prior's annexe as there weren't very many places to rent that weren't holiday lets at exorbitant prices. Greenbeck had been named as one of England's top ten most beautiful villages, and since then prices had soared and empty properties were impossible to find.

Zach tried not to notice the shine of her thick, dark brown hair, nor the intriguing fact that she had a central heterochromia that he hadn't noticed before. Her eyes were greyish blue on the outside, but dark hazel in the centre. They were so different and strange, and it made him want to stare at them more and more to note their subtle colour changes.

What on earth am I doing? Concentrate, man! She doesn't need me staring into her eyes like some wee lovesick pup!

Zach began introducing her to the admin team and Hannah gushed at them all. Smiling, shaking their hands. Laughing with them. Joking. Offering cookies. Apologising for being nervous. He noted the limp again. She favoured her right leg. He wished he'd asked her further questions during the interview, but at the time it hadn't seemed right. Maybe he'd find out more soon?

'Would you like tea or coffee, Hannah?'

'Oh, let me! Does anyone else need one?'

She bustled through to the small kitchenette and began getting out mugs and filling the kettle with water. He noticed her wince once, hiding it with a smile, and laughing at not knowing where the spoons were.

He thought he heard footsteps coming down the corridor and stepped out into the hall, spotting the new doctor. 'Dr Emery! Pleased to meet you in person at last! Let me introduce you to everyone.' He led her back into the small staffroom. 'Daniel you already know. Our HCA is Rachel, our resident vampire is Shelby, and this…' he turned to face Hannah once again

'...is our new advanced nurse practitioner Hannah. It's her first day, too.'

He stepped back to let everyone say hello to one another, and then he showed Dr Emery to her room and left her to it, going back to grab the coffee that Hannah had very kindly made for him.

'Shall I show you your room?' he asked.

'Yes, please!'

Zach led the way to the end of the corridor. Hannah's room was situated between his room and the fire exit out into the car park where the staff parked. It was bright and airy—in fact, it was a little larger than the other consulting rooms. On one side it had a desk, with computer and printer, and on the other side all the medical equipment she'd need and an examination bed, so that the two zones, administrative and medical, were separate.

'This is where the magic happens,' she said, draping her handbag over the back of the chair and trailing her finger across the desk, before opening the cupboards and seeing what was inside.

Equipment for taking blood samples, swabs, bandaging supplies for wounds. Oxygen masks and a multitude of other medical equipment that she would no doubt use on a daily basis.

'I'll just be next door, if you need to ask any

questions. Or if I'm not available Daniel is a couple of doors away. But ask anyone. You never know who might know the answer.'

'I'll do that. Thank you.'

'I guess I'd better leave you to settle in, then.'

But he found himself lingering and he wasn't sure why.

'Are you…um…in any pain?' he asked.

Her cheeks flushed red. 'Pain?' she said, as if she didn't understand.

'You seem to be in some discomfort. With your leg.'

'Oh! That's nothing. I'm used to it. Don't worry. It won't affect my work.'

'No, of course not. But if there was something I could help you with you'd come to me, yes?'

She nodded. 'Of course.'

And still he lingered.

What am I doing?

'Right, then. I'd better—'

'Can I just…?' Hannah bit her lip and stepped towards him. 'Can I just thank you, Zach, for offering me this job? I never got to say it before, and I just want you to know that you have no idea how grateful I am that you've given me this chance. I promise I won't let you down.'

And she looked into his eyes so deeply, and so earnestly, that he found himself lost for a moment. Lost in looking into those blue-hazel depths, pulled in until he suddenly realised that maybe he ought not to be.

'I know you won't. That's why I hired you.' He was lost for words, wondering why his brain seemed to have stopped working. 'Have a good morning, Hannah.'

'You too.'

He nodded and closed the door behind him, stopping briefly in the corridor to try and work out just what he was feeling and why he was feeling so out of sorts.

Her smile?

Her eyes?

Don't be a great eejit.

When the door closed behind Zach, Hannah let out a huge breath and tried to slow the rush of her runaway heart.

For three months she'd been telling herself that Dr Zachary Fletcher could not, and would not, be the handsome devil she remembered from the interview. Because her mind had been all of a fluster back then, what with her nerves from the interview, and she hadn't been thinking straight. So she'd told herself that she'd simply imagined how gorgeous and handsome he was—because no man could actually look that perfect and not be some sort of celebrity living in Hollywood, right?

Only she'd been mistaken. Zach was *exactly* how she remembered! She hadn't made him up, or imagined him, or exaggerated his looks or his accent. He was... He was...

'Exquisite. A feast for the eyes,' she murmured, squeezing her eyes tight shut and trying to tell herself that it would all be just fine...

Dr Zachary Fletcher was obviously married, and no doubt a fabulous loyal husband and father to a perfect family. And they'd have a cat and a dog, and maybe chickens or ducks in the back garden. His children would be angelic and admired by all, and he'd be the envy of all the other parents at the local school, and no doubt make everyone's mouth water when he competed in the parents' races on sports day, or helped out at the cake sale and made all the local ladies salivate when looking at him, rather than at the delectable edibles he'd have on the table before him, and they'd all be jealous of his beautiful, model-like wife...

Sinking into the chair behind her desk, she shook her head, trying to clear it, knowing she had to get into work mode, see who was on her list for the day...what she'd be tackling.

Thinking about Zach... Well, that would have to wait. Even though she knew that, realistically, she wouldn't be able to ignore him for long.

Could a man like him be ignored?

Probably not.

And he'd noticed her limp. Already. So much for her trying to hide it. His medic's antennae must have been going crazy, and she was a fool to have thought she could hide her injury from everyone here. Clean slate? Hah!

She had eight people on her list this morning. The first one due in fifteen minutes. So she took off her cardigan, hung it on the back of the door, and began to set up the clinical side of her room the way she liked it to be before calling in her first patient of the day.

Miss Petra Kovalenko came in and Hannah could immediately see what the issue was. But she didn't want to just presume.

'Good morning. I'm Hannah. How can I help you today?'

'It's my eyes. They've been really sore and itchy since Friday evening, and this morning when I woke up I couldn't open them without soaking them first in warm water.'

'I can see they look inflamed. They're very red. Are you normally fit and well?' she asked.

Petra nodded.

'Have you been around any children with eye infections?'

She laughed grimly. 'I teach in the infants' school.'

'Ah. That'll do it! I can see there's a lot of

green discharge stuck in your eyelashes, which would suggest that this is bacterial conjunctivitis. Have you had a cold recently? Earache?'

'A bit of earache…but I put that down to the sound levels at work. Children can squeal really loudly.'

Hannah smiled. 'I'm just going to check your ears and throat—is that okay?' She looked into Petra's ears using the otoscope and saw a mild redness in her right eardrum, but her throat looked clear and her tonsils were fine—as were her temperature and blood pressure.

'Okay. I'm going to prescribe you some topical antibiotics. Are you allergic to any medications?'

'No.'

'You're going to need to make sure you wash your hands regularly, as this is contagious.'

'I can still work, though?'

'Yes, you can. Just be careful with hand hygiene, and don't share towels or pillowcases at home—that kind of thing. If you start sneezing or coughing, cover your mouth with a tissue and make sure it goes in the bin.'

'I will. Thanks. When should it start to clear?'

'Antibiotics should work within a few days. If you're still getting gunky eyes after four or five days then get back in touch. But this definitely seems bacterial, so these antibiotics should

knock it right out.' She handed Petra the prescription.

'Thanks. I appreciate it.'

'No problem. You take care.'

'You too.'

When Petra was gone, Hannah let out a big
sigh of relief. First patient done! And it had been
wholly satisfactory. This was what she enjoyed
about her job. Yes, she dealt with many acute
conditions that people might consider boring,
like coughs and colds or sore throats, but she
felt as if she could do something about them,
even if it was just to reassure a patient.

She worked steadily through her list, treating
a urine infection, a migraine, a case of athlete's
foot and a painful verruca before she was able
to take her morning break. She headed to the
small staffroom and filled the kettle with water
to make some tea. As she waited for the kettle
to boil she began to shift her stance, to take the
weight off her left leg, just as Zach came in.

'Hey, how's it going? Everything okay?'

There was something about his smile… It
was so broad, so genuine. And his eyes were
so bright… And just seeing him made her have
a funny feeling in her tummy.

*It's just nerves. I just want to be liked. It's the
people-pleaser in me.*

'Yes! All good, thanks.'

'I'm glad to hear it. Just thought I'd grab a quick cuppa, and you've already got the kettle on, so...' He sank down into a chair.

Hannah smiled at him, not sure what to say. 'Do I...um...detect an accent there?'

He nodded. 'You do! I was raised in Bathgate. West Lothian.'

'Oh, really? How long were you there for?'

Zach shrugged. 'For most of my childhood. I went to Edinburgh to study medicine, and then came to England.'

'Quite a big change.'

'I guess... What about you?'

'Oh! Nothing as interesting, I'm afraid. Born in Surrey. Raised in Surrey. Worked in Surrey.' She rolled her eyes at how boring her life sounded. 'It was time for a change,' she added, hoping he wouldn't dig any more than that.

It hadn't just been time for a change. She'd needed to get away. From everyone who knew her. The humiliation had been too much to bear. She'd thought the time right after her non-wedding had been the worst, but honestly it hadn't. It had come much later, after the gossip had spread, when weeks and months had passed by and people kept looking at her with pity, as if she were the eternal underdog or something...

Her parents and her best friend Melody had all told her just to power through, but it had become impossible. She'd felt as if everyone was looking at her. Judging her from afar. Knowing every intimate detail of her life. She'd been laid bare before them all and she'd needed some privacy back. Some dignity. The fresh start that this opportunity at Greenbeck had afforded had been worth the upheaval of moving and leaving her old life behind.

Her mum had begged her not to go. Told her it didn't matter and that she should hold her head high as she'd done nothing wrong. But that was easy for Mum to say. She wasn't the one who had to face everyone and see that look in their eyes. See all the questions they had and were dying to ask. It was the worst feeling in the world.

'A change is as good as a rest, huh?' said Zach. 'Isn't that what they say?'

'Yes…' She rubbed at her left leg, trying to be casual about it, hoping he wouldn't notice.

'Everything okay?' He looked down at her leg, clearly concerned.

'I'm fine. Think I overdid it jogging at the weekend.'

Jogging? Hah! I don't jog! Why did I say jogging?

'Well, I mean… I *say* jogging… It was probably more of a fast walk. And when I say fast walk…what I actually mean is…'

She bit her lip. Her nerves were making her babble, searching for the right word, the right explanation to put him off the scent, determined not to let him find out.

She stopped talking. Chuckled. 'My leg just aches sometimes.'

'The accident?'

He'd remembered. From the interview. She was impressed. And also concerned.

'Yeah…'

'What happened? If you don't mind me asking?'

What happened ruined my life, that's what.

And she did mind. Big-time.

'I had an accident at a theme park.'

His face clouded. 'Nothing serious, I hope?'

The urge to tell him was tremendous. To just get it out into the open…not to have to hide. She was so sick of hiding. But this was her fresh start! Did she really want him knowing all about it on her first day?

She wrinkled her nose and shook her head. 'No. Just a small prang.'

Behind them, the kettle had finished boiling.

'Were you after tea or coffee?' Hannah offered brightly.

'Coffee would be great, thanks.'

'Milk? Sugar?'

'Just milk, thanks.'

'Sweet enough?' She turned as she joked, not realising that he'd got up and was standing close by.

His blue eyes were so intense! Sparkling like tanzanite. Thick, dark eyelashes emphasised their brightness. And he was such a perfect specimen of a man. Tall. Broad. Fit. His fitted blue shirt emphasised his musculature. He was... *solid*. That was a good way to describe him.

Solid, not perfect.

Exercise-conscious, not fit.

Easy on the eye, not delectable or delicious or stunningly edible!

Feeling a little unsettled by her reaction to him, she turned away, let out a slow, silent breath, and concentrated hard on making the drinks, hoping her hands wouldn't begin to tremble. She could not afford to be attracted to this guy! He was her boss, for goodness' sake! And, more than that, she'd come here to get away from men and romance and all the complications that came with them.

'I don't know about that,' he said, coming alongside her.

She made his coffee. Stirred it and passed it to him. Trying not to brush his fingers with hers and hoping that he couldn't tell that her respiration rate had increased or that her face was flushed.

'Thank you.' He took a sip. 'Perfect. Right… Back to work we go. Remember, any problems you can just come and knock on my door.'

'Yes.'

No.

She watched him go, her breath exiting her body in a loud huff once she felt he was out of earshot.

Zach took his coffee back to his consulting room, closed the door behind him and sank into his chair, rubbing his hands over his face and through his hair.

Hannah was perfectly qualified, yes, and he felt she'd fit into the small Greenbeck family as he'd expected her to, but…

What was it about her that made him long to just sit and look at her and listen to her speak for hours? She was funny. Nervous, clearly. But he was sure that was only because it was her first day.

When she got nervous she spoke quickly, and a lot, and somehow he got dragged into her orbit. He found it hard to tear himself away when she got lost like that. Wanted to see where she would take him with her stories. But…

He wasn't ready to be attracted to someone else. Not after the catastrophic failure of the relationship he'd had with Milly, the local veterinarian. He'd only just begun to hold his head high again.

Now when he saw Milly in the village, smiling and laughing, holding Hugh's hand, he was able to just drive by and not grimace too hard and wonder why he'd not been enough. And people had moved on and stopped asking him about her. Patients had stopped checking that he was okay. Life had begun to return to normal for him and he *liked* to be that way. Unnoticed. Alone. Living a simple life.

But Hannah…

Was she going to endanger the normality that he'd craved for so long? Was she going to be a wrecking ball in his life? A grenade?

Should he have hired one of the other applicants? That ANP only five years away from retirement age? Or the guy with excellent references but a terrible dandruff problem? Would that have been easier?

But, no. Hannah had made a huge impression on him. Both in her interview and in saving that baby's life. Her babbling and her smile and her sparkling personality and her wonderfully exotic eyes had dug into his psyche and refused to budge, saying, *Pick me! Pick me! Pick me!*

And so he had.

'You are in trouble,' he said to himself, clicking on the name of his next patient so that the screen in the waiting room would tell him that he could make his way to Zach's room.

As he sat waiting for Mr Mackenzie Parsons and his dodgy knee to arrive he became acutely aware of Hannah's laughter in the next room. He had to fight the urge to go and see what she was laughing at. He wanted to be a part of it, wanted to see her face light up for himself, but he knew he wouldn't. Couldn't. For self-preservation he needed to stay exactly where he was.

As if on cue, the door opened and there was Mr Parsons. Hobbling in, using his walking stick. 'Morning, Doc!'

'Mr Parsons! How are you today? Take a seat, young man.'

'Not so young these days,' his patient complained, groaning as he sank into a chair.

'How can I help you today?'

'I need you to take a look at this. I don't think it's right.' Mr Parsons leant forward, grabbed his trouser leg, and pulled it up over the most swollen, red and inflamed knee Zach had seen for a long time.

His eyebrows rose. 'Okay… How long has it been like this?' he asked. He wheeled his chair forward to examine the knee, gently palpating the joint, exploring it, trying to feel for the underlying structures beneath the swelling and the infection that had clearly set in.

'Started Saturday night.'

'As bad as this?'

'No, no. Just an ache then. But Sunday morning... Ooh, it really began to hurt, and I've been popping paracetamol since. My daughter wanted to take me to A&E—but I didn't want to bother them with this.'

'I don't think they'd have thought you were bothering them, Mack. Did you bang your knee in any way?'

'I did some gardening Saturday morning. Pruning back some climbing roses that had got out of hand. My Matilda had let them run wild and free in her garden for years. They were a mess and she finally let me at them.'

'Did you catch yourself on any thorns?'

'Maybe a little. Just there—look.' He pointed at a small puncture hole to the right of the kneecap that looked dark and purple.

'I see it.'

Mr Parsons' knee was hot to the touch. Most definitely an acute infection had got in. Maybe complicated by some cellulitis, too.

'We need to get you on some antibiotics. Do you still have a full range of motion in the leg?'

'Oh, yes. It feels a bit stiff, like, but I can move it.'

'Let's take your temperature... Any chills? Sweats?'

'Now you mention it, yes…'

'Nausea?' Zach reached for his digital thermometer and placed a new disposable cover on the tip before placing it in Mack's ear.

'No.'

It beeped. His temperature was raised, and Zach didn't like it. He feared that this might be a case of septic arthritis and knew that Mr Parsons needed to be put on an antibiotic drip.

'This isn't good, Mack. Especially with your artificial knee joint. I'm sorry to say I think you need to receive those antibiotics in hospital. Is there anyone who can take you to A&E? Your daughter Matilda?'

'She's had to go to Southampton today.'

'Right. Then I'm going to ask Reception to call an ambulance for you. I want you to go straight there. It probably means a bit of a stay, I'm afraid.'

Mr Parsons nodded his head. 'I thought it might be the case. Well, you know best, Doc. As long as I can go home first to lock up?'

'I'll just go and have a chat with Reception. Get them to ask the ambulance to pick you up from home within the next two hours?'

Mack nodded.

'You stay here a moment.'

'Will do.'

He went to ask one of the ladies on Reception

to order an ambulance for pick-up from Mack's house in two hours, and gave her Mr Parsons' medical details so she could provide them to the ambulance service. Then he returned to his consulting room.

'All done. When you get home, I want you to keep that leg raised up on a chair—understand?'

'Yes, Doc. I do. And thank you for taking the time to see me. I appreciate it.'

'No problem. And next time go straight to A&E with something like this. Please don't wait.'

Mr Parsons nodded.

'When did you last take painkillers?'

'About three hours ago.'

'Right…'

He ended the consult and began to write up Mack's notes. He feared that Mack might need surgery to replace the artificial joint, depending on how bad the infection actually was, but no one could know at this stage. He hated it that Mr Parsons might now have a long road in front of him just because he'd decided to tackle some overgrown roses.

But that was how life was. Sudden, unexpected events could overtake you at a moment's notice. Even if you'd been in a relationship for over a year with someone and felt secure at last, life had a way of spoiling everything…

When the notes were written, Zach called for his next patient, hoping that the rest of the day would be uneventful, but no sooner had he sat down and begun to make a start on his admin tasks did an alert pop up on his screen. Dr Emery, their new GP, had an emergency on her hands.

He dropped everything and went rushing to her room, to discover that her patient, Sarah Glazer, was about to give birth unexpectedly.

'What can I do?' he asked Stacey. He didn't want to step on her toes. This was her patient. But he also understood that this was her first day here, and she might be overwhelmed, so he would help in any way she needed.

'Call an ambulance.'

'I'm on it.' he disappeared back to Reception. 'Charlotte? I'm going to need you to call another ambulance.'

'Two in one morning? Are we going for a record?'

'Maybe! It's for Sarah Glazer—she's on Dr Emery's list. Tell them she's about to deliver a baby and we'd appreciate an emergency ambulance as quick as they can.'

He went back to Stacey's room and saw that now Daniel was there with her, helping her, and knew he'd only be in the way.

'Daniel? I'll take your last patient so we can clear the surgery.'

He went to Daniel's room and explained to Mrs Robotham why he was stepping in. She didn't seem to mind, so he went through the rest of the almost completed COPD review that Daniel had been doing and then sent her on her merry way, with the promise to see her again in a year's time.

'We'll call you—don't worry.'

'Thank you, Dr Fletcher.'

As he headed back into the corridor he met Hannah, who was watching as Sarah Glazer was wheeled on a stretcher from Dr Emery's room.

'It's all go here, isn't it? So much for a quiet little village surgery.' She smiled.

'Absolutely. We may be small, but we are mighty!'

Her smile lit up her eyes, and briefly he found himself staring again. Deliberately he followed the paramedics outside, just to give himself some space from the gorgeous new advanced nurse practitioner.

He checked to make sure that Dr Emery was okay, and asked if she needed to chat, but she said she was fine, that it was all in a day's work, and he was reassured that he'd made the right choice in choosing her.

When he got back inside the surgery Hannah was making everyone a hot drink. 'I think we all deserve it,' she said, as all the staff filed into the small staffroom for lunch now the front doors had been locked.

He went to help her. Show her where the trays were. But when he bent down to get them out of the cupboards so did she, and somehow they banged their heads together.

'Ow! Are you okay?' he asked.

She was rubbing at her head. 'I think... Yes. I'm okay.'

'Let me check.'

He reached for her head, let his fingers slide into her soft hair as he checked to make sure there were no breaks in the skin, or any bumps, but she seemed fine.

She looked up at him, her eyes meeting his, and he let go, stepped back, feeling his cheeks colour. 'You're all right.'

Him, on the other hand... Not so great.

He pointed at the low cupboard. 'Trays are in there...on the side.'

'Thanks.'

'I'll leave you to it...unless you need a hand?' She looked a little pale.

'I'm fine. You go and sit down. It sounds like you doctors have had a busy morning.'

He smiled at her, and then sat down so that he had his back to her. This confusion he was feeling over Hannah…it needed to stop. He didn't want it. Or need it. It was a distraction when he needed to be clear-headed, to help his two new staff members settle into their jobs on their first days.

Both he and Stacey had needed to order an ambulance. It happened… There'd been a day last July when the surgery had ordered three ambulances in the course of a few hours! A suspected heart attack, a severe asthma attack and a woman he'd suspected of having suffered a stroke. They probably wouldn't need an ambulance now for days…weeks… Or maybe they'd need another tomorrow? Who knew?

Being on the frontline of primary healthcare, you never knew who might walk through your door. A patient might think that they were just having a bad headache—they wouldn't know that perhaps they were having a transient ischaemic attack, or TIA, which was a mini stroke. They might come in complaining about a pain in their leg and discover that they had a deep vein thrombosis. A clot which might prove dangerous. Some patients played down their ailments. Others exaggerated them. It was what they faced day to day.

Hannah came past him and stooped to lay the tray of tea-and-coffee-filled mugs onto the table. Her cookies were nearly all gone. Just one or two left on the plate. Did he want to try one and be blown away by her baking skills, too?

He noticed her wince and rub at her left leg again, but chose not to mention it. She'd say if there was a problem.

She sat in a chair opposite and picked up one of the mugs, sighing with satisfaction after taking her first sip. 'That's lovely.'

'How's your first day going, Hannah?' asked Charlotte from Reception.

'Good, thank you. How is it on Reception?'

'Busy. But we're lucky we can offer more appointments now that you and Dr Emery are here. We've had to turn people away or make them wait, and not everybody understood that we simply couldn't fit them in.'

'I hope people weren't too mean to you?'

'There'll always be one or two bad apples who try to make life difficult, but thankfully the people of Greenbeck are understanding. And everybody knows everybody, so they really can't get away with being rude or horrible.'

Hannah smiled and nodded, sipping from her mug.

Zach had his lunchbox in the fridge, and now that Hannah was nowhere near the vicinity of it he went to fetch it. Then, with his mug of coffee in hand, he went back to his consulting room to eat in private.

He couldn't sit in that room with her. If he did, he'd want to look at her. Ask her loads of questions. And the poor woman was trying to have lunch. It was her first day, and she'd be trying to make a good impression on everyone. She didn't need him prying too.

No, it was best if he ate alone. It wouldn't be seen as strange. He often ate in his room. He'd done it a lot after his relationship with Milly had broken down. So many people had wanted to ask him questions and he'd just not wanted to deal with it. Not right away. Not when it was all so raw.

Sighing, he put down his sandwich and picked up the phone, dialling a number he knew off by heart.

'Hello?'

'Evelyn? It's me.'

Evelyn McDonald wasn't his real mum. But she was the woman he'd given that honorary name to. Evelyn was one of the many foster parents he'd lived with growing up in Bathgate, and the only one with whom he'd stayed in touch. She was kind and gentle, and she'd taken him in when he was fifteen and got him through his school exams before he'd been moved on elsewhere.

'Zachary! It's been so long. How are you?'

'Not bad. Thought I'd check in.'

'Okay. Normally when you call me to just check in, there's something going on. Do you need to talk about it?'

'No. Aye. Maybe…' He leaned back in his chair, running his hand through his hair. 'It's just one of those days, you know?'

'Is it Milly?' she asked quietly.

Evelyn had never been keen on Milly. It was as if his foster mum had had a sixth sense about her not being right for him from the beginning.

'No. It's not her.'

'There's someone else?' she asked, surprised.

'No.' He shook his head, thinking of Hannah.

'Oh. I thought there might be.'

'No. I've had two new members of staff start today and it's been a complicated morning, that's all. There's a lot of expectation on a first day.'

'Are they nice?'

'The new staff? Aye. They're bonny. A new GP who's come down from Scotland, actually, and a nurse from Surrey.'

'Mm-hmm. Single, are they?'

He laughed. 'Yes, but it's not like that. One's a single mum and the other…' He couldn't think of how to describe 'the other' without giving anything away.

'I understand. Look, Zach, you've been on

your own for some time now. No one would blame you if you started noticing someone else.'

'I'm not noticing someone else!' he protested.

'Okay, I believe you. Maybe.' He heard her chuckle. 'But if you like this nurse, then…why not?'

'Who said it was the nurse?'

'You did…when you paused.'

'Evelyn, You see and hear too much that isn't there.'

'Och, it's there, laddie, you just can't admit it yet.'

He shook his head in exasperation. 'How are things there?' He paused. 'Were Lachie's bloods good?'

There was a sigh. 'Not bad. They're letting him start chemo again, so that's bonny.'

Lachie, Zach's foster father had recently been diagnosed with brain cancer. They'd discovered a large tumour after he'd begun complaining of excruciating headaches and dizziness, but his chemo had been stopped for a while after he'd developed an infection and been admitted to hospital. Fate had not been willing to give the man an easy time of it, and had allowed him to contract C Diff whilst he was in there. Clostridium Difficile was a bowel condition that caused pain and extreme bouts of diarrhoea.

'Good. And you're both okay?'

'Apart from that, aye. I saw Mrs Fincham the other day and she sends her best wishes to you.'

Mrs Fincham had been his science teacher at secondary school. 'She was a good teacher,' he said.

'She was.'

'Well, I'd better get on. Lunch breaks only last for so long.'

'Okay. Well, you take care. And remember— you can call me just to check in and say hi. You don't have to wait for a reason.'

'All right.'

'And, Zach? Be kind to yourself. You're worth it.'

He smiled. Evelyn knew him well. He was his own worst critic.

Wishing her goodbye, he got off the phone and finished his lunch. His drink had gone tepid and he needed another one before afternoon clinic started, so he headed back to the staffroom, expecting it to be empty as everyone prepped for the afternoon shift.

And it was—except for Hannah, who clearly thought she was alone as she sat with her head bowed, as if in pain, and rubbed at her left leg.

'Hannah?'

Her head shot up and her cheeks flushed bright red. She tried to hide the movement of rubbing her leg, pretending to straighten out her trouser leg. 'Oh! You surprised me.'

'You're in pain.'

She screwed up her face and wrinkled her nose, as if what he'd just said was Grade A ridiculousness. 'What? No!'

She moved to stand, but as she put weight on her left leg she winced and sucked in a breath.

He was at her side in a heartbeat. 'What is it?'

'It's nothing!'

'You're wrong. It's clearly something. Now, you're either going to have to tell me or I'm going to insist on having you examined.'

Hannah bit her lip. 'By you?' Her voice quavered.

'I could. But if you'd prefer a female doctor to check you over, I'm sure I could get Dr Emery to take a look.'

Hannah sighed, closing her eyes before looking up again. 'No. It's bad enough that you'll have to know. I don't need everyone knowing about it. This is so embarrassing... And on my first day as well.'

'Pain isn't embarrassing. Let me know how I can help you.'

She nodded. 'Okay, but I don't want anyone else to know. And it's probably best if I show you...' She looked away, seeming almost embarrassed.

'Only if you're sure.'

'I am. But…not here. Could we go to your room?'

Intrigued, he nodded.

Even though he offered his arm, she told him she wanted to walk unaided to his room. She was clearly limping, and when they got to his room she grimaced and went to the examination bed, pulling the curtain across for some privacy.

'You remember I mentioned an accident?' her disembodied voice called from behind the blue curtain.

He did remember. 'You said you had a prang at a theme park.' He began to wash his hands, just as something to do.

'Yes. That's right. Well, it was more than a prang.'

'I kind of guessed.'

He was pacing slowly, back and forth…back and forth, his mind racing. Had she had leg surgery? Maybe her bones had been pinned? Comminuted fractures could be terrible injuries to recover from. Perhaps she was missing some muscle? Or had had skin grafts?

He heard her get onto the examination bed. 'You can come in now.'

He stared at the curtain, suddenly incredibly anxious. 'Okay…' He stepped forward, pulling open the corner of the curtain and trying not to show on his face any reaction to what he'd *not* expected.

Hannah had a mid-thigh prosthetic.

She was an amputee.

CHAPTER THREE

'I WAS ON a roller-coaster. It was a new thrill ride. It had only been open a few months and I was keen to try it. But the braking system failed and we ploughed into a stationary car ahead of us. I got my legs trapped.'

More than anything, she'd not wanted to reveal this. Some people changed once she'd told them she was an amputee. They looked at her differently. Or even, as in one particular case, dropped you like a hot potato because you didn't fit the image of the hot fiancée he'd prided himself on having any more.

Zach, to his credit, didn't let any shock cross his face. He simply nodded. 'Are you having phantom pains?'

She shook her head. 'No, it just feels really sore around the socket.' She pulled it free of her leg and noticed that the liner she wore inside had folded over. That was what had begun to cause an irritation. 'Damn it!'

'Here…let me.' Zach gave her room by placing the prosthetic on the floor and then examined the skin around her upper thigh.

She tried not to flush at the fact that he was touching her upper leg with his bare fingertips. Or the fact that he was being so gentle and nice. Or that, this close, he smelled like a summer breeze.

Zach probed the reddened skin. 'There's no sore, but the skin is irritated. I'll put a dressing on it to help protect it.'

'I can do that,' she said, feeling that she'd revealed more about herself than she'd ever wanted to on her first day, and not wanting him viewing her as helpless.

But he stopped her. 'Stay where you are. Sit back. I can do this. I don't very often get to play around with bandages. Why should you nurses have all the fun?'

He winked at her before bending to pull out drawers and look in cabinets, but came up empty-handed.

'Bandages are in *my* room,' she told him. 'Cupboard under the sink.'

'Hmm… You're right. Stay there. Don't move.'

He glanced at the clock to check the time and so did she.

They had about five minutes before afternoon

clinic started. If she gave him two minutes to find the right bandage, another minute to put it on and the last two minutes to get her prosthetic back on, then she might be able to start her afternoon clinic on time. She didn't like to run late.

As she waited, she gazed around his room, but saw nothing that gave any clues about his personal life. No photographs of family. No model wife. No cherubic children. Not even a picture of a beloved pet. There was no relaxing art on the walls—just good health posters and information about flu, shingles and Covid jabs.

Zach Fletcher was a mystery man. Or just a private one.

Doesn't make any difference. He's just a colleague.

The door to his consulting room opened and he came back in, smiling broadly, his arms full of supplies. 'I wasn't sure which would be best...'

'That one.' She pointed at a packet to the left, keen to get this over and done with. It was exposing, her sitting there. What if someone walked in?

'Ah. Thanks.'

After opening the packet, he began to apply the dressing to her leg, relieving the pressure on her irritated skin. 'How's that?'

'Not bad. We'll make a nurse of you yet.'

He picked up her prosthetic, checked the lining wasn't folded this time, and helped her place it back on.

'I'll let you get dressed,' he said.

He left the bed area, pulling the curtain over for her privacy again, even though he'd just seen her without her trousers on and might even have noticed her knickers. Black. Sensible. Comfortable. She'd stopped wearing sexy knickers after the accident, having not felt sexy since.

Flushing, she adjusted her clothing and shifted off the bed and back onto both feet, testing the leg to see how it felt.

It did feel better.

Pulling the curtain open, she saw him at his desk, his back to her.

'Thank you, Dr Fletcher.'

'It's Zach. And the pleasure is all mine.'

No. She couldn't call him Zach right now. Not after he'd seen her exposed like that. Limbless. In sensible knickers that her mother might wear. He had to stay as Dr Fletcher.

'Well, I appreciate it. I'd better get off and start my afternoon clinic.'

'Okay.'

'And you promise not to tell the others?' she asked.

He made a zipping motion across his mouth. 'Patient confidentiality.'

But she wasn't his patient. Not really. He'd helped out a colleague.

She left him to his clinic.

It was a strange afternoon. Zach got through it, like he did any other day, but he couldn't help thinking about Hannah and what she had gone through.

She'd been through a terrible trauma. Life-changing. And yet she remained optimistic and bright and funny.

And beautiful.

He'd be lying if he told himself he hadn't noticed that. He'd noticed it on day one, but it had not factored in his decision to offer her the job. She'd simply seemed a good fit for Greenbeck. But by obtaining this good fit for the surgery, had he made his own life incredibly complicated?

Already he was questioning himself. Worrying about her. Why had she not told him about the accident properly before? Probably because she didn't know him well enough to share something so personal. But had she felt she might be discriminated against if she had? He hoped not. He wasn't that type of guy. Wasn't that type of employer. Or was it more to do with the fact that people often hid facts from him? Patients lied every day. Milly had lied to him...

She had told him once that she loved him, but that had been untrue because she'd been sleeping with someone else. Hugh. Someone he'd considered a friend. He'd found them together and even then, in that moment, with the evidence right before his eyes, she'd tried to lie. Hugh had tried to lie. Said it meant nothing. Told him it wasn't what it looked like. Had they thought him stupid?

He'd never discovered the truth about his own parents, either. Evelyn had said his mum hadn't been able to cope with him and had placed him into care when he was two years old. He had no memories of his biological mother. And apparently his father had never stuck around and there'd been no other family.

He'd been cast adrift in the world as a child *and* as an adult. Alone. Unloved. Abandoned. So it had remained easier to stay on his own. To be the best doctor he could be and care about people in a professional way. Without risking his heart.

Evelyn had told him he shouldn't have to live that way. That he deserved love and that one day he'd find happiness with someone. But he wasn't sure he could trust anyone enough for that any more. He could live without love. Hannah could live without a leg. People went without all the time and it was fine.

There was some leftover chilli in his fridge at home, from the day before, so he began to bake a large potato in the microwave to go with it, and stood there, staring at it, watching it go round and round, his mind wandering through an imaginary theme park.

Picturing a crashed ride and a crushed leg.

And the hot salty tears that must have run down her face because, being a nurse, she would have known what her injury must mean.

'*Start!* Start, you stupid thing!'

Hannah had been at Greenbeck for two weeks and had really begun to feel like part of the family already. Everyone was so lovely. So kind. Welcoming and warm. And apart from the blip with her prosthetic on that first day with Zach, no one else knew and everything had gone perfectly.

Until now, when her car wouldn't start to take her back home for the evening.

The engine sounded dry and croaky every time she tried to turn it on. It made vague attempts to sound as if it was desperately trying to start. A couple of times she even thought that luck might be on her side as it nearly caught, but then it just died on her, and when she turned the key an array of lights lit up on her dashboard.

She had no idea what they might mean. She could diagnose a urinary tract infection, prescribe medication and bandage the worst of diabetic leg ulcers and help them heal—but diagnose what had gone wrong under the car bonnet? Understand what all those orange and red lights meant?

No chance.

She smacked the steering wheel in frustration, then jumped when someone rapped their knuckles on the passenger window and bent down to look into the car.

Zach.

Her heart was thumping fast, because he'd scared her, and his warm smile merely accelerated it further.

She got out. 'I think it's died on me. Do you know car CPR?'

'I've not taken that particular training course. You're going to have to call the breakdown people. Unless you want me to take a look at it?'

She raised an eyebrow. 'You know how to fix cars?'

He bobbed his head left, then right. 'No, but I could pretend, if it would make you feel better.'

She laughed, and bent down to find the lever that popped the bonnet. She had no idea what she was looking for either. Walking to the front of the car, she watched him lift the bonnet up, set the catch to hold it in place and then have a good look. Touching different bits. Checking the oil. Making a lot of humming noises as he thought.

'Any clue?'

He turned to look at her. 'Not at all.'

She laughed with him. 'I guessed as much.'

'I strongly suspect that cars might be more complicated than people. Especially since they all run via computer chips these days.'

She nodded. 'I'll call the breakdown service.'

'Want me to wait with you?'

'Oh, no, you don't have to do that. You must have plenty of things to do.'

'It's no problem. It wouldn't seem right, just leaving you here on your own. Listen—why don't we go over to The Buttered Bun? They're open till late today. We can grab a cup of coffee and you'll be able to see the breakdown guys arrive if we sit by the window.'

Sitting with Zach? In a café? Away from work? Like…friends?

She could think of a million reasons why not, but just one look at his twinkling eyes and his cute yet oh-so-friendly smile and she just couldn't say no.

'Sure. Why not?'

She locked up her car and they made the short walk across the green to the café. A sign on the door stated that tonight was the Knit and Natter group, and anyone was welcome. When they went in, they waved and said hello to a group of smiling middle-aged and elderly ladies and one gent, who were all working their magic with pointy needles and a variety of wool, before grabbing a window seat.

'Just coffee?' Zach asked.

'I'm a bit peckish. I'd love a sandwich if they have any left?'

'I'll check.'

She watched Zach go to the counter and talk to the young lady behind it, who had the same stunning red hair that their new GP Dr Emery had. It was almost as if they could be sisters.

'No sandwiches left, but Jade says she can do you a toasted currant bun?'

'Perfect. Thanks. You must let me pay.' She stood up to get some money out of her purse, but Zach held up his hands.

'No, no. My treat.'

Hannah settled back down into her seat. He was being very kind—which wasn't helping with her attraction to him. If he was prepared to sit and wait with her, did it mean that there was no one at home waiting for him? She'd overheard a couple of the receptionists mentioning the name 'Milly' alongside Zach's the other day, but she hadn't caught the whole thing. Nor did she want to get embroiled in workplace gossip. But she kind of wanted to know if he had someone. Because she didn't want this to look like something it shouldn't.

Right now she had no certainties, and it left her feeling on edge around him. Nervous. Because she liked him. A lot. Something she'd not taken into consideration when she'd applied for a new job.

Zach brought over the tray. A mug of coffee for her, a small teapot for him, and two hot toasted currant buns for them to share.

'Looks great.'

The wonderful aroma of the sweet toasted bun alongside that of melted butter made her mouth water.

'Tuck in.'

She took a bite and made a pleased sound of satisfaction, then dabbed at her mouth with a napkin. 'So, do you need to call anyone?' she asked. 'Tell them you'll be late home?'

'No.'

'Oh.'

Shoot.

'You?' he asked.

'No.' She took a sip of her coffee. It was hot and strong and almost burned her tongue.

He raised an eyebrow. 'How are you enjoying being at Greenbeck?'

'Oh, I love it! It's just what I needed.'

'Are all your family back in Surrey? Do you miss them?'

'They're not far… Only an hour or so away.'

But she didn't want to talk about herself. He already knew far too much.

'What about you?' she asked. 'So far away from home in Scotland.'

'Ah, well…' He smiled, clearly considering how much to tell her. 'I don't actually have any real family. There are some foster parents I still speak to when I can. I ought to arrange some time to go back and see them, but you know how it is. You get busy…'

'You do. So…you were in care?'

He nodded.

'What was that like?'

'Not the greatest barrel of laughs, but it taught me a lot about life. About what's important.'

'Life lessons are important. I know *I've* undergone a few.'

'Your leg? That must have been quite an adjustment?'

She nodded. 'Something like that. I felt lonely a lot. Like no one else could understand what I was going through. At least until I joined a support group. That's why I'm always keen to establish them at my place of work. Having a chronic illness or injury can be isolating.'

'You're right. I felt a similar thing when I was at school. Everyone else seemed to have parents and families and places to go at the weekends. Birthday parties and huge family Christmases and Hogmanay celebrations. Me...? I went back to the children's home. And even though there were always other kids there, it was one of the loneliest experiences of my life.'

'Well, aren't we a couple of Cheery Charlies?' she said, and smiled.

He laughed.

She took a sip of her drink.

'I've learned from it, though,' she went on. 'I've learned that I used to waste so much time, waiting for the *right* time, but there's no such thing. Whilst you're waiting—whilst you're being afraid—time is slipping through your fingers. You need to take action. Go after what you want and stop waiting for everything to be perfect.'

'What were you waiting for?'

She looked away from him. Where were the breakdown people? Why weren't they here yet? Did she really want to tell him this?

'I was waiting for myself to be whole.'

Zach frowned. 'How do you mean?'

She sighed. The fight to hold back was so

easily lost when she was with him. It was dangerous.

'I was engaged when I had my accident. The wedding was only a month or so away, so we pushed it back. Initially the doctors thought they could save my leg, and I had three surgeries whilst they tried. Then infection set in and they needed to amputate. I told Edward to push the wedding back further, which he gladly did. In fact he seemed relieved by my decision, which should have been a red flag, but I was too busy focussing on my recovery. I thought we would get married when I had learned to walk unaided with my prosthetic. I visualised his reaction to seeing me walk down the aisle all by myself. I romanticised it. I thought he'd be proud of me. Realise just how much he loved me. But it turned out that Edward was happy to push the wedding back because he wasn't sure he could be married to an amputee. He said he loved me, but wasn't *in* love with me, and that physically he didn't fancy me any more. He sent a text on the morning of our wedding, to say it was over.'

Zach had exactly the right reaction. He frowned, looking angry on her behalf, and also incredulous that anyone could react in such a way. 'What an idiot,' he said. 'Sounds like you had a lucky escape.'

She smiled sadly. 'I didn't think so at the time.'

'I know that feeling. If it makes you feel any better, you don't hold any exclusivity on terrible past relationships.'

'I'm glad. What happened with you?'

Zach took in a big breath and sighed. 'Her name was Milly. *Is* Milly. She's the local vet—no doubt you'll run into her at some point. We were together for a year…got engaged. Everything seemed perfect.'

'What happened?'

'We were so busy planning our wedding we forgot to talk about what we wanted from our marriage, and when I did ask Milly informed me that she didn't want children. *Ever.*'

'And you do?'

He nodded. 'I've never had a family. Not a blood family. When I was young I always held on to the fact that when I became an adult I could start one. It's hugely important to me. And Milly had seemed perfect for me until that little bombshell. I tried to work it out with her. Asked her if there was any chance she'd change her mind in the future…'

'And there wasn't?'

'No. There didn't seem to be any wiggle room at all. I tried. I hung in there. Seriously considered not having children myself and thought Milly would be enough for me. I told myself she would be. But things had changed between us. There was tension. An atmosphere. She told me that she would always feel guilty for not giving me what I wanted—and then I found her in bed with one of my friends, so that was the end of that. And it didn't take long for the news to get around in such a small place as Greenbeck.'

'I'm sorry.'

'Don't be. Like you, I had a lucky escape. I didn't think so at the time, but I do now.'

It was astonishing to Hannah that someone would have cheated on him. And even more amazing to learn that he was single. So…both of them single people. Both looking for love.

She shivered at the thought. It was actually a little terrifying. Upsetting too. Like Zach, she'd dreamed of settling down one day and having a family of her own. But who would she find to love her without seeing the great empty space where her leg ought to be? And what about the fact that her prosthetic represented the emotional baggage that she carried with her everywhere?

But Zach would have the chance to find someone else, right? He had been nothing but kind and welcoming. He was warm and friendly. He took time for people and was clearly a dedicated doctor who wanted the best for his patients. And he'd helped her with her prosthetic. Done everything humanly possible to make her feel comfortable about him seeing it. He'd come to her aid when her car wouldn't start, and now he was sitting with her, keeping her company until the breakdown service arrived.

He was a gentleman, and as far as she was concerned this Milly had made a terrible mistake in letting this man slip through her fingers.

Zach's attention was suddenly snagged by something out of the window. 'Oh. They're here.' He pointed over to her car. The breakdown service had arrived.

'Oh, right. Well, thank you for keeping me company. And for the hot buns.' She smiled, realised what she'd said, then blushed madly. 'I mean—'

He laughed. 'I know what you mean.'

When he smiled the way he was doing now— truly smiled, broadly, widely, his eyes crinkling at the corners, shining bright—he was the most handsome man she had ever seen. She could have stared at him all day.

'Why do I keep saying silly things in front of you?' she asked. 'It's like my brain stops working.'

And then she blushed some more, because she

wasn't sure if she'd just admitted something to him that she shouldn't have.

But if he thought so, he didn't let on. He let her off the hook, standing up and waiting for her to follow. 'It's fine. But I'm not going to leave you yet. What if they can't fix it? You'll have no way to get home.'

Now she was scrabbling. He made her nervous. He made her say stupid things. She would much prefer it if he went away.

'You've done more than enough already. I can't ask you to waste more time waiting around for me.'

'It's not wasted time. Making sure you're all right is important.'

She thanked him as they made their way out of The Buttered Bun and walked over to the staff car park next to the surgery.

She explained the situation and the breakdown woman popped the bonnet and started running some diagnostic tests.

Hannah leaned back against the low stone wall next to Zach and gave him a friendly nudge with her elbow. It was the safest way she could think of to touch him.

'You're a good man, Zachary Fletcher. I hope you don't let this Milly take up too much room in your head.'

'I don't. Like I said, I've learned from it.

There'll be someone out there who's perfect for me—who wants the whole shebang. Marriage, kids…grandkids one day. When I'm ready to trust again. And no doubt there'll be someone out there who is perfect for you, too. We've just got to be open to it when they show up.'

'Absolutely.'

'Mind you, with my track record I'm not sure I'll be all that great at trusting anyone. And if the trust isn't there…' He shrugged, indicating that such a relationship would be likely to fail.

'I know what you mean,' she said. 'It's a huge risk, isn't it? Putting yourself out there… Making yourself vulnerable…' Her voice cracked on that last word and she swallowed down tears. She'd not thought she'd be so emotional, but Zach had opened up her emotions like no one had in a long time. It was weird and strange and terrifying.

'Then perhaps we should make a pact?' he suggested.

She wiped away a stray tear. 'A pact?'

'Yes—an agreement.'

'About what, exactly?' she asked, amused by the turn of their conversation.

'Earlier, you said everyone needs to stop waiting for the perfect time and the perfect person. But we both know we're going to hold off until we feel…ready. The dating world is full of imperfect people and perhaps it will never be the right time for us both to get back out there. Perhaps we need to somehow practise in a safe way? To grow our confidence? Make sure that neither of us dates the wrong person or ignores any red flags? Maybe we can teach each other how to find love and happiness with someone who truly adores us without question and wants exactly the same things as us.'

'Oh? As simple as that, huh? Okay. How do we do that?'

'We date each other.'

'I'm sorry—what?' She almost choked.

Zach laughed at her reaction. 'Hold your horses! I'm not saying we actually *date* each other. I meant we practise being *on* dates. Together. That way, if one of us does something wrong, or ignores what could potentially be a red flag, the other one can point it out with no recriminations and no hurting the other person.'

'Oh…' Well, that didn't sound too bad. 'Like an experiment?'

'We'll test hypotheses. See what works. What doesn't. Then, when someone perfect for us comes along, we'll be so well prepared we won't lose them, and they'll think we're amazing because we will have trained ourselves to be.' He smiled. 'What do you think?'

It was a crazy idea! Ridiculous! But it was

tempting, too…because what if he was right? What if he could help her feel like more than she was?

'I think you might be on to something.'

'Great. We're both adults, so we know what we're doing, but we've also both experienced abandonment, which can really screw a person over. So we promise to make sure that the other person gives love a chance when it arrives. You can be my guinea pig and I'll be yours.'

She nodded. That sounded just fine. Being each other's test subject meant that she wouldn't actually ever go out with him, right? It would just be practice. To see how they came across on dates. And it didn't sound as if he was interested in *her*.

'Cool. You've got yourself a deal.' She held out her hand and he shook it, smiling.

But this was too close to him…with those smiling eyes and that gorgeous grin. And touching him…

She broke the contact and stared at the mechanic as she analysed Hannah's car. Eventually she signalled them to come over.

'I'm afraid it's your alternator. It's completely dead and isn't sending out any electrical signals, so your battery is dead, too. I can replace the battery, but not the other. I'll call out a tow lorry and have your car taken to the local garage.'

'Barney's?' asked Zach.

The woman nodded.

Zach gave Hannah a lift back to Mrs Micklethwaite's. When he'd parked up, he looked at her awkwardly. 'So…when should we start our experiment?'

She shrugged. 'Maybe we should start as we mean to go on? No messing about. No waiting for the perfect time to start before we get cold feet. This weekend?'

He nodded.

Much later, she slumped onto the bed in her room, telling herself she'd done the right thing, agreeing to a fake date. They were going to meet at the pub. They'd agreed it was a perfect first date location. Public. They would eat. Drink. Talk. Play darts or pool. Maybe go for a walk later…

They both deserved to find love.

To find the one.

What was the worst that could happen?

CHAPTER FOUR

Mr Jerry Fisher sat down opposite Hannah and reached into his pocket, pulling out a piece of paper.

Oh, no, he's got a list.

'I'm experiencing some dizziness. Room-spinning stuff.' His thumb moved down the paper. 'And I get tingling, and this foggy feeling, and sometimes it takes me a long time to find my words.'

She glanced at his medical file. Jerry was eighty-two years of age and was always at the doctor's with a string of mild complaints. He'd been in yesterday to see the HCA to have his earwax removed. A couple of days before that he'd been in complaining about ringing noises in his ears.

'Okay… I can see you have a list there,' she said, 'and we only have a short time together, so why don't you pick the two most important things that are bothering you and we'll go from there.'

'They're all bothering me, though.'

'I know…' She reached forward and held out her hand for the list.

He passed it to her.

'There are *twelve* items on this list, Mr Fisher, and I have only ten minutes with you. It's just not possible for me to provide you with the most effective care if I try to cover them all at once.'

'But what if they're all connected?'

She glanced at the list. 'With the greatest of respect, I don't think a blackened toenail and a suspicious mole are connected. You do seem to be having a lot of trouble with your ears, though. Let me look at those.'

Hannah glanced at his ears, using the otoscope, but could see absolutely nothing wrong. The eardrum was as it should be after treatment from the HCA. No extraneous wax. When she checked his temperature it was perfect, and so was his blood pressure.

'Is there a chance, Mr Fisher, that…well… that you may be a little lonely?'

Jerry looked down at the ground and she knew she'd hit the nail on the head.

'Things just haven't been the same since Beryl died.'

'That's your wife?'

He nodded. 'I just wanted to speak to someone. I'm sorry, Nurse, for wasting your time.'

He got up to go.

'Mr Fisher—wait.' She laid her hand on his arm. 'Loneliness can be a serious issue, and if you're creating medical complaints just to have someone to talk to here, I'm assuming that you're doing this elsewhere?'

He looked at her, shamefaced. 'I go to the library and ask them to order me books I don't want. I go to the local shop just so I can talk to the girl on the checkout. She's nice. And often I'll sit in The Buttered Bun and nurse a coffee all day, just to be around people.'

'Don't you have friends? Family?'

'They're all gone. I was the youngest of my family and I've had to bury them all. Beryl's family, too. The friends I used to have are either dead as well or in care homes.'

Hannah felt terrible for this old man. But she had a solution.

'I just may have the answer to your problem, Mr Fisher. I've recently started a support group here at the surgery for people like yourself, who are looking for companionship and friendship. And the best bit is that I've teamed up with a local dog rescue centre, who are prepared to bring over some of their long-term residents so that you can sit and play with the dogs, or maybe take them for a walk through the woods up to the castle.'

'Really? I used to have a dog… I've felt too old to take on another one.'

'Then this is ideal. Shall I put your name down? They meet once a week, on Saturdays, just after lunch.'

'Yes, please do.'

She smiled. Jerry Fisher looked brighter already. Just the thought of having some companionship was enough to put a sparkle back in his eyes.

'If you do have any serious health niggles, though, Mr Fisher, you'll need one ten-minute slot per issue, okay? I'd be happy to see you again.'

'You've been very kind. And understanding.'

'It's my pleasure. I know what it's like to feel alone.'

'A young thing like you?'

'You'd better believe it.'

'Will you be at this friendship group?'

'Yes, I'm going to come. As the organiser, I want to make sure it's working.'

'Then I'll look forward to seeing you, Nurse. Thank you.'

'Take care, Mr Fisher.'

With her patient gone her clinic was done for the morning, so she performed a few stretches to get the kinks out of her back and for just a moment sat in her chair, in her room, enjoying the peace and quiet.

She closed her eyes, hoping to meditate for a moment or two. But all she could think of was her upcoming practice date with Zach.

They'd not really established any rules. Did they have to treat it like a proper date and get dressed up? Or could they just be relaxed and test each other with questions over a pint of beer and a packet of crisps?

She was going to be at the new support group first, with the patients she had identified as lonely. She could hardly turn up to that in a little black dress…

On Saturday morning she was nervous. She'd arranged to meet the dog rescue people and the companionship group outside the surgery, as they couldn't have animals inside the practice, and as lunchtime passed she saw a group of about eight people begin to gather, amongst them Jerry Fisher.

At that moment a van pulled into the car park, emblazoned with the logo of the local dog rescue centre, and two women got out. They were both young and blonde, one with her hair up in a high ponytail, the other with hers down.

'I'm Dee—this is Elle,' said the one with the ponytail.

'Hannah. Great to put a face to the name,' Hannah replied.

'We've brought a variety of dogs. Smaller and older ones, mainly. Not likely to pull.'

There were spaniels and cockapoos, a York-shire Terrier and a West Highland White, and soon everyone was partnered up with a dog.

Hannah was walking a King Charles Span-iel named Fudge, and she led the group towards the public footpath that would wind its way up through the woods towards the castle. She knew they probably wouldn't actually make it that far. It was quite a steep climb, by all accounts. But she'd been told by Shelby, the phlebotomist at the surgery, that there was a path that led off the main one and remained level, leading in a large circular route, taking in a small lake.

She noted that Jerry had the Yorkie, and a big smile on his face as he chatted with an older lady by the name of Pearl.

'This is lovely,' said Dee. 'I've not been out this way before.'

'Where do you live?' Hannah asked Dee.

'Near Beaulieu.'

'Oh. Isn't that where the motor museum is?'

'That's it.'

'Are you into cars?'

Dee laughed. 'No. Not my thing. I much prefer dogs.'

Hannah nodded. 'It must be lovely in your job…when you get to see a dog connect with a family and find a new for ever home?'

Dee smiled. 'It is. It makes me want to wave a magic wand over them all, so they'll all get a new family and a loving home, but the world doesn't work that way, does it?'

'No. And if we had something like that, I think we humans would use it on ourselves first.'

'Ain't that the truth? Imagine finding another human who would totally adore you and be loyal to you for the rest of your life. Think it can be done?' Dee laughed.

'Probably not.'

And that was why she had to do this practice dating with Zach—because if she thought it truly was impossible to find someone who could love her and be loyal to her, then perhaps *she* was the one who needed training and re-educating?

She refused to acknowledge the strange feeling that came over her when she considered her date with Zach. The discomfort… The desire to call him and cancel… Because it didn't matter what she felt. Hannah was not going to get involved with anyone again.

She wasn't whole. She wasn't complete. Who would find her attractive now, with an entire leg missing and a thigh stump that had healed oddly so there was a weird dimpled scar on the end of it? Even she could barely look at it sometimes. Why would any man? Edward certainly hadn't wanted to know, and he had loved her, so...

Zach had seen it, of course. She tried to forget that. The way he'd put his carefully composed doctor face on when he'd seen she was an amputee. She recognised that look. All medical professionals had it. It was a carefully curated look. One you used at work to show that nothing a patient showed you could shock or appal or make the patient feel embarrassed in any way.

He'd worn that look.

What must he have really felt?

Thought?

It doesn't matter. We're just practising. It doesn't mean anything. I'm just his test run for when the real thing comes along. And I'll be happy for him.

CHAPTER FIVE

ZACH HAD OFFERED to walk his neighbour Marvin's German Shepherd dog, Rebel, whilst Marvin was in hospital. Marvin had called him to ask if he could let Rebel out into the back garden to do his business, and feed him morning and night, but Zach loved dogs and so had offered to take Rebel for a proper walk, if Marvin was okay with that?

'Sure thing—if you don't mind? They're saying I can come home tomorrow.'

'No, it'll be good for me. Don't you worry about Rebel. I'll keep him with me until you're home. I'm not on call this weekend, so it's easy for me to keep him with me, fed and watered.'

'You're a good man, Zach.'

'So are you, Marvin.'

He'd decided to take Rebel up to the castle and back. He knew that Hannah was taking her social group there, with the rescue dogs, and they were supposed to be meeting later for their first practice date. He figured she'd feel more comfortable if he was dressed in casual dog-walking clothes, too.

He wasn't sure why he'd suggested this fake dating thing. Maybe it was because he'd not liked the way Hannah had kept her injury from him. That had niggled slightly. Clearly she had some issues in her past, as everyone did, but he didn't like secrets and he'd always thought he was the type of person others could be honest with. And if he wanted a perfect working team at the surgery, then he needed to be honest with her. So he'd opened up about his own pain with Milly.

When he'd heard about Edward, Hannah's ex, and how he'd treated her a rage had built inside him and he'd wanted, desperately to show Hannah that she was worth someone's time and effort. She was important. Not worthless. Which was how this Edward had obviously made her feel. It would be his duty, hopefully as her friend, to help her heal. So he'd offered to help her find love again. He wasn't doing it for himself. He wasn't ready to find love at all. But he'd play along until she found someone.

It was a decent distance to the castle and would be a great cardio workout—going up that hill and back again. He usually jogged up to the castle, so it was nice that today he'd taken his time to get up to the castle, to calm his nerves and go exploring down paths he didn't normally take. There was a pretty bridle path that took him past the edge of a sheep farm, and a field with a mix of donkeys and horses that he hadn't even known was there. Rebel seemed interested in them all, and wagged his tail excitedly every time he saw a horse up close.

Zach checked his watch when he began to feel hungry, and realised he ought to head back down to Greenbeck so he could meet Hannah later, go to the pub and get something to eat.

As he and the dog strolled down the hill he enjoyed the relaxation of just being present in nature. A dappled light glinted through the verdant foliage, and the earthen floor was scattered with small sticks and old pine cones that Rebel occasionally picked up and carried in his mouth, before dropping to go and sniff at something more interesting.

It felt good. He'd always wanted a dog, but had never got one as he didn't think it fair to leave it cooped up all day whilst he was at work. Maybe one day, when he found the right woman to settle down with and they began their family, getting a dog was something they could discuss?

It was easy to hypothesise when it wasn't actually happening. When he really tried to imagine it—finding someone, trusting someone—he got a little nervous.

As they got to the bottom of the path he became aware of voices and saw a group of people walking dogs. He heard laughter and conversation and knew he'd come across the social group.

Hannah's group.

He felt his heart begin to race and a smile crept across his face almost without him realising. He raised his hand in a wave, saw Hannah smile and wave back, and could not explain the feeling he experienced at that.

The others began to wave too.

'Dr Fletcher!'

'Hey, Doc!'

Rebel happily greeted all the other dogs, and there ensued a lot of wagging tails and sniffing of butts.

'Hey, how's it going?' he asked Hannah.

'Great. I didn't know you had a dog,' she said in surprise.

He laughed. 'Oh, I don't. This is Rebel—he belongs to my neighbour. I'd love a dog, but with the hours we work…' He smiled at her, loving how relaxed and happy she looked. He wasn't used to seeing her in normal clothes. She normally wore her uniform. But today she looked amazing. A sleeveless white blouse, fitted blue jeans, boat shoes… And her dark brown hair was loose and flowing.

'Zach? This is Dee. Dee—Zach. Dee has helped me set up this group for some of our patients.'

He shook Dee's hand. 'Pleased to meet you.'

Dee was pretty, and the way she was looking at him, eyeing him up and down, gave him the feeling that she liked him. It made him feel a little nervous.

'Pleased to meet *you*, Zach.'

He nodded, and then extracted himself from the conversation by putting Rebel back on his lead, clipping him on securely.

They began walking again—out of the woods, into the lane that led to the surgery car park.

Dee and Elle got water bowls out for all the dogs to take a drink before they loaded them back into the vans. Hannah was giving everyone hugs and thanking them for coming and telling them she hoped they'd show up again next week.

Dee and Elle said their goodbyes and promised to see Hannah next week, and then they were gone, too.

'Just us, then. And Rebel,' she said, scooting low to give the dog a head-rub.

'Are you hungry yet?' he asked.

She looked at him. 'Actually, I am.'

'Still up for the pub? You could back out, of

course, but I would point out that it's not good behaviour to back out when you've made a date with someone.' He grinned.

'Okay. And you should know that women often have second thoughts about going on a date, but often push through just to give the guy a chance.' She smiled sweetly. 'Let's go to the pub now. Sit in the beer garden. There'll be shade and water for Rebel.'

'Sounds good to me.'

The Beck Canal ran along the bottom of the garden at the Acorn and Oak pub. There were ducks, geese and swans meandering about on the grass, or gliding smoothly across the water's surface, whilst people sat chatting on wooden benches and occasionally threw crisps onto the ground for the birds to eat.

'How's your car?' asked Zach.

'Back up and running again, thank you. For a while there I contemplated buying a pushbike to get around, but Barney managed to fix it.'

'A bike's a good idea. I've got one. There are some good trails around the village and this area. I could show you.'

'Oh. Actually, that sounds interesting. I ought to do more exercise, and it does seem silly to drive to work each day when I could bike it in probably the same amount of time.'

'What sort of bike would you be thinking of? Racing? Mountain?'

'I haven't thought about it. Though I guess one suited for roads as well as off-roading on trails?'

'A mountain bike, then.'

'Perhaps.'

'I could come with you. Help you pick a good one. If you want.' He shrugged and took a sip of his beer.

Hannah appreciated that he was trying to help. But spending more time with him looking at bikes... Going out on rides together... Would that be too much? Probably not. He was just doing it as a friend—he wasn't interested in her in any other way.

'Thank you...that'd be very kind.'

'Don't mention it.'

Wow. He had such a wide, generous smile. It truly lit up his eyes and made them sparkle, and in turn made happy feelings twirl in her gut. He was just so...

What was the word?

Gorgeous. There. She'd admitted it. Zach Fletcher was gorgeous. The most attractive man she'd ever met. The kind she could fall hopelessly for. The kind she could just sit and stare at for hours with a dreamy expression on her face and...

Dear God, am I doing it now?

'This bike shopping thing,' she said. 'And going on rides together. That would be as friends? Or as part of our practice dating?'

'Friends, for sure. I don't think taking a girl bike-shopping would be her idea of a good date.'

'Gold star, Dr Fletcher.' She smiled.

Thankfully, the server arrived at that moment, bringing them the cod, chips and mushy peas they'd both ordered from the menu. It looked perfect. Thick-cut, twice-cooked chips, beer-battered cod and a small pot of mushy peas topped with mint sauce.

'Thanks.' Hannah picked up her knife and fork. 'This looks good.'

'It does.'

For a brief moment they ate in silence, tucking into their food.

'You must have been very happy with the way your group went?' Zach said eventually. 'Lots of people showed up.'

'I am. I'm hoping that once word spreads it will get bigger, and people who wouldn't normally talk to one another will.'

'Those dogs were great.'

'They were good as gold. Like Rebel, here.' She smiled at the German Shepherd, who sat by their table, hungrily watching each mouthful they devoured.

A couple walked past them and sat down at a far table. Hannah noticed Zach's face change. It had lost some of its sparkle.

'Everything okay?' she asked, glancing at the couple.

'Milly and her new beau.'

'Milly? As in...? Do you want to go inside?'

'No. Of course not. It's fine. It's just...'

'A little in your face?'

He nodded and took a sip of his drink. 'It just niggles because she wasn't honest with me. I thought we had a truthful relationship and we didn't. So... End of, really. Sorry—I shouldn't be talking about an ex on a first date.'

She leaned in. 'Are you kidding? Bashing exes is the fun part! You get to explain to your date all the ridiculous stuff that they did, and then you bond and laugh together and promise not to be like that.'

'Are you sure?'

He was looking at her so intently that it began to make her second-guess herself.

'Well, I'm not sure now... Perhaps that's where I've been going wrong? Okay. No talk about exes. Especially not on a first date. We save the horror stories for when we know a person better. How does that sound?'

'Better.' He took another sip of his cold beer.

'This finding happiness lark is complicated, isn't it? Full of potential minefields.'

'You're telling me... I once went on a date with this guy and he...' She trailed off, blushing. 'On second thoughts...that's a horror story, too.'

Zach laughed. 'See?'

'Absolutely!'

She ate a chip, looking at Zach, her mood thoughtful. Did a first date really want to hear about her horrible history with men? She'd thought they did, but maybe they were being polite? She didn't want Zach to relive his upset with Milly. The betrayal. The lying. The deceit. Nor did she want to imagine him with her.

Looking at Milly, at first glance Hannah thought she was beautiful, and could understand why Zach might have fallen for this long-legged blonde sylph. But when she stopped to look properly Hannah could sense a meanness to her features. Her eyes were too sharp. Small. Dark. Her lips were too thin. There were too many angles to her face, and she pouted a lot as she listened to her companion.

Milly glanced over now. Saw her sitting with Zach. Curiosity crossed her features and then she turned back to her companion and laughed.

Hannah wanted to see Zach happy more than anything. Not reliving his past. If she saw him happy, it would give her hope that maybe one day she could have happiness, too.

So, who would be her ideal man?

Someone tall and dark-haired, like Zach? With that tousled look. Blue eyes. They always looked nice with dark hair. And a broad, genuine smile that made his eyes sparkle and twinkle. Someone kind and considerate. Clever. Someone who made her laugh. Someone she could talk to and just be herself. Someone who shared the same values as her. Someone who loved animals and wanted pets. Someone who didn't care that she was incomplete. That she was an amputee. A man who saw her for who she was, and not just a woman missing a leg. A man she could just sit and shoot the breeze with in a pub. A man who made her feel warm and fuzzy inside. Who could make her heart race. A man who made her think she could do anything.

Like Zach…

Zach. I've just described Zach.

She put down her knife and fork and dabbed at her mouth with a napkin. 'Could you excuse me for a moment?'

'Of course.' He stood when she did. 'Gentlemen do stand when women get up to leave?'

She nodded. 'I just need the loo.'

He nodded and she hurried away to the ladies' room, face flaming with the sudden reality of the fact that Zach exactly fitted her description of the perfect guy.

Physically, maybe. In character, perhaps. But what was he like in a relationship? He was still showing her his good side. Maybe there was another?

He was her boss. Her colleague. And she wasn't ready to fall for anyone else. She'd agreed to this fake dating thing knowing that, and was only doing it because she wanted to help Zach find someone and be happy. She wasn't ready to do that *herself.* Couldn't bear the idea of experiencing all those emotions again…developing feelings for someone only to have him cast her aside, like Edward had.

I have a lot to offer someone—I know I do. But what if I'm found wanting?

She would not allow herself to fall for Zach. Because, if she was being honest with herself, it would be easy to do so. Zach was extremely easy on the eye, he was incredibly warm and friendly, and he was funny and clever and handsome and…

Oh, dear Lord, he's all the things!

She felt cowardly. But she was protecting herself. She'd given her whole heart to Edward and she'd thought he'd be there for her after the accident. She'd wanted to show him how grateful she was for all his support. She'd wanted to learn to walk up the aisle unaided as a surprise on her wedding day. She'd been so excited about it! All those hours of practice…imagining his face when he turned to see her…the way his face would light up. Perhaps he'd cry?

But no. Instead she'd received that text from him on the morning of their wedding, telling her that he didn't want to get married, that he wasn't in love with her. That he just couldn't get past her amputation.

'I'm sorry. I can't do this. It's over.'

He'd given her no chance to ask questions. He'd simply turned his phone off.

She'd thought that maybe they could just postpone the wedding if he wasn't ready…get married later, perhaps. But no, again. Edward had moved on quickly. And now he had a girlfriend who was tall and leggy and fun. Someone who didn't need to remove her leg and prop it up against a wall at night before bed.

The devastation he'd left in his wake…the loneliness he'd left her with…the feelings of inadequacy…

No. She couldn't go through all that again. Couldn't risk putting her whole heart on the line again. Because she wasn't sure she had a whole heart any more, and any man—most especially Zach—deserved a whole heart being given to them.

That was why she was doing this. For him. Because he'd been so kind.

Hannah splashed water on her face, dried it with a paper towel, then headed back outside, feeling apprehensive. As she neared the table, she saw that Zach was on his phone.

'Aye, that would be great…okay. See you then. Bye.' He clicked off the phone and smiled at her as she returned. 'Tell me—is it good etiquette to take phone calls from the person you call your mother during a date?'

She laughed. 'Hmm… I don't know. Maybe. It depends on the reason for the call. If it's an emergency, then obviously that's okay. If she's ringing to tell you some good news, then that's also okay. But if she's ringing to tell you that you mustn't be home late and she's already laid your clothes out for you tomorrow morning… Probably don't mention that to your date.'

He grinned. 'Then I'm okay. She was ringing with good news.'

'That's great.'

'Am I allowed to share it with you? What's the protocol on that?'

'You can tell me if you want to. I guess it depends on how you think the date is going and whether or not you like the person.'

'Hmm… Well, let me see… I do want to. I

think the date is going well and right now I do like the person,' he said, with a grin.

Were his cheeks reddening? she thought. He was trying to hide it by taking a long drink of his beer. Dutch courage?

She blushed herself. 'Then please share. I'm all ears.'

'My foster father got through his chemo this week without any adverse side effects and he's going to ring me tomorrow.'

'Chemo? What type of cancer is he fighting?'

'Brain.'

'I'm so sorry. What stage is it?'

'Three.'

She nodded. 'Do you want to talk about it?'

He shook his head. 'Maybe later. I'm mindful that I don't want to drag down the date by bumming everyone out talking about illness and death.'

She nodded. 'Good call. For a practice date, of course. But as a friend I'm here any time you want to talk about it.'

Her own grandfather had died from cancer. For him it had been lung cancer that had metastasised. She barely remembered him—only snippets—but she did remember the toll it had taken on her mother. Cancer was difficult for all the family.

They suddenly became aware of panicked

voices behind them and both turned. An elderly couple near the canal were staggering to their feet. The old man was struggling to breathe, his hands blindly shooting out and knocking over his drink. The glass smashed as it rolled off the table and hit the paving slabs beneath it.

Ducks scattered wildly and his partner, the older woman, shouted. 'He can't breathe! Some-one help!'

Hannah and Zach leapt to their feet and raced over.

The man was having some sort of asthma attack. A serious one. He was already on the ground, weak from not being able to get enough oxygen.

As Zach attended to him Hannah called for an ambulance. When the paramedics arrived they checked the man out, placing a nebuliser and mask over the man's face. The man—Don-ald—began to breathe a little easier.

After the excitement had died down, and the man was on his way to hospital, the landlord of the pub gave Hannah and Zach a free slice of cheesecake each. It was banoffee cheesecake. Rich and decadent.

'Never a dull moment when you're a medic,' Hannah said.

'No, there isn't.'

'And, you know, saving someone's life when

you're on a date kind of makes them think that you're an amazing hero.'

'Not sure what the ethics would be in always having someone on hand to get into a medical crisis for you to solve... Probably dubious and best to avoid.'

Hannah laughed. 'Agreed! Unless it happens naturally.'

'Good point. Now, should I offer to walk you home?'

She nodded. 'That would be gentlemanly and nice—thanks.'

He smiled. 'I'm trying my best.'

CHAPTER SIX

IT WAS WEIRD, walking side by side with Zach and the dog. They walked slowly, taking in people's gardens, admiring flowers, waiting for Rebel to sniff various posts and garden gates, and it felt as if she was walking with a boyfriend.

Only normally if she walked with a boyfriend she'd hold his hand, or have her arm around him, but she couldn't do any of that with Zach. Technically, this was only a first date. And a practice date. Not even the real thing. So she stuck her hands in her pockets as it felt the most comfortable thing to do with them.

Up ahead she spotted Dr Emery, with her son Jack, coming towards them.

'Hey…' Hannah greeted them.

'Hi! What a gorgeous day, huh?' said Stacey. 'We're off to feed the ducks.'

'Sounds good,' said Zach.

Hannah crouched down to make eye contact

with Jack. 'You must be Jack?' she said. 'I've heard so many amazing things about you from your mum.'

She'd also heard some horrible things. Stacey had told her that they'd come here after some bullying that Jack had experienced at his previous school, due to the large birthmark he had on his stomach.

Jack looked intrigued.

'She said to me that you're the best reader and the bravest boy she knows,' Hannah went on.

'I do like to read.'

'Me too! Perhaps you could recommend some books to me one day.'

Jack nodded shyly.

She stood and smiled at Stacey. 'How's he settling in?'

'He's doing all right. I'm trying to think of ways to help him feel he fits in more. Daniel suggested scouts, but I'm not sure...'

'That would be *great* for him. He'd enjoy that.'

She looked down at the little boy. He was cute. Freckled, with the same red hair as his mum. She hated to think that he felt isolated and different. She knew how that felt.

Her sympathy for what he was going through suddenly made her brave. She addressed the little boy again. 'Hey, Jack, want to see something cool?'

Jack nodded.

'I've got a super-secret that makes me special and unique. Want to see it?'

'Sure.'

She raised her trouser leg to reveal the prosthetic, glancing at Stacey with a smile.

'Whoa…' Jack was fascinated.

'I lost my leg a short while ago. It changed my life. Made me think that everyone was staring at me. But you know what? They're not. People are so worried about themselves, they're not thinking about you or me. Once, I hated what had happened to me. I was very sad. But now… It's a part of me. It's what makes me special and different and I'm *better* for it. It showed me who my true friends were. So, if you ever want to talk I'm here for you, okay?'

Jack nodded.

Hannah looked at Stacey, who mouthed *Thank you*.

'Shall we go and find those ducks, then?' she asked her son.

'See you Monday,' said Zach.

Stacey and Jack said goodbye, and then they were alone again. Zach kept looking at Hannah, smiling broadly.

'What?' she asked.

'That was a good thing you just did for that little boy.'

'Well, I know how it feels to be different. To feel that you're not as good as everyone else.'

'You know you are, though? Miles better.'

She blushed at his compliment. 'Thanks.'

'I mean it.'

'Well, you're very kind. And I mean that.'

They walked a little further. Getting closer and closer to Mrs Micklethwaite's.

'I guess I should ask…is getting my prosthetic out on a first date the right thing to do?'

'Why not? But you don't have to show them. You could tell them about it, and if they have a problem with it then it's best to know sooner rather than later, right?'

She nodded, reaching down to scratch behind Rebel's ear. 'That's for sure. But what if it freaks them out?'

She remembered coming round from her amputation surgery. Slowly opening her eyes to see her family gathered around her bed, all of them happy, smiling. Except Edward, who'd looked as if he was really struggling with what had happened.

'Then you'll know they're not for you. Honesty is the best policy—isn't that right?'

'Yes. You're right. Okay… Rule number one

for me, then, is to be upfront. Tell them about my leg.'

'It doesn't need to be the first thing you speak about.'

She laughed. 'Maybe not. *Hi. I'm Hannah. I'm an amputee. Want to look?* Yeah, I agree... it doesn't come across as romantic, huh?'

He shook his head with a smile, and then they were back at Hannah's place. They stopped at the garden gate.

'Well, this is me. Thanks for the meal.'

'You're welcome. I enjoyed it.'

'You're probably sick of the sight of me. You see me all week, and now we've met at the weekend...'

'Are you sick of the sight of *me*?'

She looked at him. 'No. I'm not.'

'Then ditto.'

Hannah laughed. 'What's the protocol for ending a first date?' she asked nervously. 'Shake hands? Peck on the cheek?'

She had to force herself to stop giggling nervously. Because even the idea of kissing him on the cheek was...

Oh, my God. I can't even describe what that would feel like!

'I guess...if it's gone well and you like them and you feel comfortable...a peck on the cheek is reasonable.'

'And if you like them a lot?' she asked.

Were her cheeks red? They felt red. Hot. Flaming. Was there a colour hotter than red?

'Then a short kiss on the lips would be acceptable,' he replied, his face flaming also as his eyes met hers.

Then he gave an embarrassed laugh that was oh-so-endearing, and she looked away because she couldn't meet his eyes.

'Okay. Should we do the kiss on the cheek thing, then? We're just practising, and I think it would be...' she swallowed hard '...*awkward* if we did anything else.'

He nodded thoughtfully. 'You're right.'

Smiling, he leaned in and she proffered her cheek.

Or that was what she meant to do. But something right at the last moment changed her mind, and she turned instead and their lips met.

His lips were soft. He smelt good.

Heart pounding madly, she couldn't believe what she was doing! Kissing Zach on the lips?

She opened her eyes as he pulled away in surprise, and laughed and shrugged. 'It was a good date. And I like you,' she tried to explain, cheeks still blazing with heat.

He stepped back, a little uncertain. 'I guess those were the rules...'

Now it seemed awkward.

She chuckled nervously. 'I'd better get in. Lots to do,' she said, stepping away regretfully, but trying not to show it by grinning madly.

'Yeah, I'd better get back,' he said, indicating the path behind him and beginning to walk away.

Why did this feel like the end of a real date? *Why?* She found her gaze dropping to his mouth, eyeing his lips, and found herself laughing nervously again.

'Enjoy the rest of your weekend, Zach.'

'Yes. You too. But you're going to have to go inside. I'm not leaving until you are. That's what a gentleman would do. So you should watch for that. When you're dating for real.'

'Yes! When it's for real. Right. That's good. That's good advice.'

She gave him a small wave, lifted the latch on the gate and headed for the front door. She rummaged in her bag for her key and unlocked the door, then stepped inside, turning at the last moment to smile and wave one more time before closing it.

When the door had closed, she felt a long, low breath escape her and she fell against the door, face pressed hard against the wood. It was cool and smooth and she wanted to stay there and never move—yet she also had to fight the urge to unlock the door, fling it open and rush back outside.

Instead, she lifted her head and peeked through the small glass window in the door shaped like a diamond. She saw that Rebel was looking up at Zach, head tilted to one side, as if to say, *What are you doing? You missed a trick there.*

'What would you know?' she heard him say, glancing at the house one last time and then walking away.

Hannah's next patient was a seven-month-old baby brought in by her dad, who'd noticed some lumps and bumps. She smiled in delight as Mr Asher walked in with his daughter, who was in her pushchair, kicking her legs and holding on to a cuddly plush horse.

'So this is Amy?'

The dad sat down. 'Yes.'

'And how can I help you today?'

'She's been a little off for a few days, and then this morning, when I was changing her, I noticed these little raised lumps. They look like blisters.'

'Okay. And is she normally fit and well?'

'Yes.'

'I can see from her record that she's had all her vaccinations. Is she eating and drinking?'

'Drinking fine, but she's a little off her food.'

'Okay… And is she urinating as usual. Filling her nappy?'

'Yes, that all seems the same.'

'All right, I'll just check her temperature.'

Hannah slotted the thermometer into the baby's ear and pressed the button. It beeped back a reading that informed her that Amy did have a slightly raised temperature.

'Let's take her over to the bed and you can show me these bumps.'

She let the dad undress his daughter whilst she washed her hands at the sink. Then she donned gloves and went over to the examination bed to coo at the baby and gain her trust before she did her examination.

She didn't like to traumatise babies if she could help it. If she could establish a good rapport with her younger patients they would sense that she wasn't someone to be feared. And even though Amy was only seven months old, and would not remember this visit at all, she still wanted to make this experience comfortable for Amy.

'Hello, there! Oh, look at you! *Look* at you! Aren't you adorable?'

She could see the lesions on the baby's skin, clustered mainly around her mid-section, her armpits, her nappy area and legs. Hannah tickled her slightly to make Amy laugh and then shone a light into her mouth.

'You're such a good girl! Oh, yes, you are.'

She straightened and placed her stethoscope in her ears and listened to Amy's chest whilst smiling at her and wiggling Amy's arm, as if she was playing.

'Thanks. You can get her dressed now.'

Hannah removed her gloves, washed her hands again and settled down in her seat.

'Amy has chicken pox.'

'Oh, the poor thing.'

'Yes. She's going to feel a little uncomfortable for a while, and she'll be infectious until these blisters began to scab over. It's probably best to keep her away from people—especially vulnerable people—and don't go near any pregnant mothers.'

'I wonder where she's caught it from?'

'You don't know anyone with the virus? She's not at nursery, or a childminder's? Anyone in the family?'

'No. Yesterday we took her to a baby massage group, because we thought with her being grizzly it might help. Could she have got it there?'

'It sounds like she already had it, if she'd been a little off. If you have the number of her baby massage group you ought to give them a call and inform them, so that the other mums and dads can be alert for an outbreak.'

He nodded. 'I will. Sounds like I've got my own little Typhoid Mary.'

Hannah smiled. 'She has a few spots in her mouth. That's probably going to put her off her food, if her mouth's sore. Just give her plenty of fluids, infant paracetamol if you think she needs it, and you might want to make sure you keep her fingernails trimmed so that she doesn't scratch. You can use mittens or socks on her hands at night.'

'Okay.'

'You can use calamine lotion to help with the itching. Or there are other soothing creams you can get from the pharmacist. If you speak to them, they can advise you on what the best topical application is to use.'

'Thank you.'

'When you bath her just use cool water, not too hot, and when you dry her don't rub her with a towel, just pat her dry. That'll help. And use a moisturiser or lotion afterwards.'

'Got it.'

'And if you have any concerns or worries, or you think she's getting worse, then give us a call and we'll see her for another check-up, okay?'

'Perfect. How long do you think she'll be like this?'

'Maybe five days or so?'

He sighed. 'Long time for a little one.'

Hannah nodded. 'She'll probably cope with it a lot better than you will. Parents naturally worry, but it's good for her to get it now. Saves her from having a bad case as an adult.'

'True. Okay, thanks, Hannah.'

'You're very welcome.'

She smiled as they exited her room and began to type her notes into the system.

Little baby Amy had been an absolute delight. Hannah loved babies, and hoped one day to have her own. But she couldn't see that happening for a while. For that to happen she'd have to be serious with someone, and she couldn't imagine that happening yet either. She'd have to find someone she could open up to. Someone she could be vulnerable with. Someone who didn't care about her missing leg. Someone who wanted the same things out of life as her. Someone who could make her smile and laugh...who gave her warm feelings.

Zach's smiling face came to her mind and she pushed it away.

Again.

He'd been in the forefront of her thoughts a lot just lately and that couldn't be good. Since that date at the weekend she'd felt that...well, that he was amazing! But she couldn't fall for him, right? He was her boss. Her colleague. She'd just started here. Getting into another relationship doomed to failure was not the way to go.

They were practising for *his* benefit, not hers, that was all, and she had to keep telling herself that time spent with Zach was only borrowed. One day he would feel comfortable enough to ask a woman out, and it wouldn't be her... So be it. Maybe she should try to quicken the process and get it over with? Or, maybe, considering how he'd made her feel since that day, she should avoid having another date with him for a little while?

No. A long while.

'Do you have any balloons?'

Zach's ears pricked up. He'd recognise Hannah's voice anywhere.

He was in the Greenbeck village store. A place that had been run by the Riley family ever since he'd been there. George and Lucinda Riley had been stocking it with the same stuff for years. Bread, milk, fruit and veg, tinned goods—that kind of thing. But recently he'd noticed a few different things creeping into their stock. Things that he strongly suspected were down to the current member of staff behind the counter—Stephen, their youngest son.

There were postcards now. Calendars featuring Greenbeck. Touristy bits and pieces. Keychains. Sunglasses. SIM cards! He'd been talking about trying to bring his parents into the twenty-first century and it looked as if the tide was beginning to turn. And Stephen had grown fond of telling every customer, 'If it's not on the shelf, I can order it in.'

Zach had popped into the store to pick up some dog food for Rebel, whom he was still looking after. He'd used up what Marvin had had left in his cupboards, and he'd also needed something for his own meal that evening. Stephen might not have persuaded his parents that Greenbeck was ready for fresh pasta in the shop yet, but he'd found some dried farfalle, some fresh chicken, bacon, cream and a single lemon.

Now Hannah's voice drew him out from the shadows at the back of the store like a moth to a flame. 'Hello again.' He placed his wire basket of goodies on the counter next to hers.

Her smile of greeting was genuine. 'Hello! What are you doing here?'

'Same as you, I imagine. Shopping.' He looked at the contents of her basket. Cheese. Sausage rolls. Crisps. 'Having a party?'

'No, but Shelby will be. It's her birthday bash this week, remember?'

'Oh, that's right!' Shelby was their phlebotomist. 'You must have drawn bringing the snacks?'

She nodded. 'And the decorations. Because Anna on reception is poorly, so I said I'd pick them up for her. What did you draw?'

'Non-alcoholic fizz.' He pointed at a couple of bottles behind the counter. 'Three of those please, Stephen.'

'Can do.' Stephen filled his basket.

'So...balloons? Streamers? Anything like that?' Hannah asked Stephen.

'I can get you some.'

'When?'

'Tomorrow. Come by after work.'

'Perfect. Just those, then, please.' She indicated the snacks, and the sad-looking pre-made sandwich, the single packet of crisps and the bottle of water.

'I hope that's not your dinner?' Zach asked.

'This?' She laughed and blushed. Paused. Nodded. 'Actually, it is. Mrs Micklethwaite is having a family dinner and won't have time to cook for me, so...'

'Why not come to mine? I've got more than enough for two. Chicken farfalle. What do you say?'

She smiled at first. Seemed to think for a while. For a very brief moment he feared she would say no. Part of him *wanted* her to say no. It would let him off the hook. He'd not been able to stop thinking about her lips since the weekend and it was extremely distracting. And their practice date had been terrifying. But one look at her sad little meal and the invitation had just rolled right out, before he could stop to analyse what his mouth was saying.

'Just dinner. And maybe you can help me walk the dog afterwards.'

'You've still got Rebel?'

'Marvin's developed some complications. They're keeping him in.'

'Oh. Poor Marvin. Nothing serious, I hope?'

'He spiked a fever, so they're just taking precautions.'

'Right. Well, that's sensible.' She glanced at her sandwich. The lettuce looked a little droopy. The cheese a little plastic. The tomato a little mushy. 'Fine. Okay. Dinner… What time?'

He swallowed. 'Oh. Um…about six?'

'Sounds great.'

Stephen had finished ringing up her purchases. She paid him, said goodbye to the two men, and left.

Zach watched her go, before turning back to a grinning Stephen.

'Just dinner?' he asked, with a raised eyebrow.

'Och, get away with you. She's a colleague, and anyone would have done the same thing.'

Stephen nodded. 'Sure! Absolutely.'

Zach shook his head as Stephen chuckled. Once his items were in the bag Zach had brought from home, he hefted them from the counter.

'Just don't forget to order her stuff,' he said.

Stephen saluted. 'Yes, sir.'

What had she agreed to? She'd not thought about running into him at the village store! She'd thought Zach would shop away from the village, at a large superstore, or something. Not there. Anywhere but there.

And now she had agreed to go to his place for dinner.

Was this part of their practice dating thing? She wasn't sure. But he hadn't said anything about it being a date so she decided she would make it absolutely clear that it wasn't by dressing really casually, not bothering with make-up, and generally being…what? Friendly? Casual? Colleaguey? Was colleaguey a word? Probably not, but that was what she would be.

She glanced at the clock. Five-fifteen. Forty-five minutes before she had to be at his house. She stood in front of her wardrobe and began pulling out clothes. Dress? No. She didn't often wear dresses anyway—what the hell were these doing in her wardrobe still? Tossing them to one side, she began looking at her blouses. The blue one was nice. It had that frill. But that was too feminine, and she didn't want him looking at her and being reminded that she was a woman. T-shirt? Hmm...

She pulled out a claret T-shirt. It was plain. Not too tight. And—oh, yes!—khaki linen dungarees. They were casual. Covered her figure. And they were comfortable. There was even a small bleach stain on the leg that said, *You're not important enough to make me want to dress nicely for you.*

Good. That would do. Trainers as well.

Dressed, she sat in front of the small mirror that she'd perched on top of the small bedroom table. Hair up? Or down?

Down is probably best.

She grabbed her cleansing wipes and began to remove her make-up, eliminating every last trace. Her earrings were removed too. She automatically reached for her perfume, then stopped. No, this was an anti-date.

Hannah stood in front of the mirror, turning this way. That. She looked as if she was about to start painting and decorating a room. Which was perfect.

'Good. Nothing about me screams, *Be attracted to me!*'

She was about to leave the room when she suddenly thought she ought to take a gift to

Zach's. If you turned up for dinner, wasn't it polite to take something? A bottle of wine?

I'll have to buy one on the way.

Hannah set off at a casual pace to Zach's. Walking seemed best. She didn't want to get there too early, and she could waste some time perusing the wine.

When she got to the village store Stephen was still behind the counter. 'Hi,' she said.

'Hello,' he replied. 'Twice in one day! I must be popular. What can I get for you?'

'I need wine.'

He grinned. 'Don't we all? Is this for dinner with the doc?'

She felt her face flush. 'It's just a meal. I don't want to arrive empty-handed.'

'Well, I happen to know that Dr Fletcher likes this one.' He swept a bottle from behind the counter, presenting it to her almost as if he were a sommelier. 'It's his favourite and would go well with the chicken.'

He took a step in front of her, smiling. She perused the bottle, considering. If she turned up with his favourite wine, what would that say? She decided not to take any chances, shook her head, and said, 'How about that one?' She pointed at another behind the counter.

Stephen shrugged, picked up the other bottle. 'Sauvignon Blanc. Good choice.'

'Thanks. How much?'

She paid him and walked out of the shop, happily feeling that she'd dodged yet another bullet. It was a decent bottle, but it wasn't his favourite, so he wouldn't think that she'd been asking about him at the shop. He'd view it as a casual choice. Nothing important. It was vital to Hannah that he did not think she was interested in him.

'Because I'm not. I'm not. *I'm not*,' she muttered to herself as she lifted the latch on his gate and sucked in a strengthening, empowering breath before knocking on his door.

Inside, Rebel barked, and she smiled. The dog would be a good buffer. Because right now she felt like a small fly, about to set foot on a giant spider's web. This was Zach's home. His territory. Hardly neutral ground. He'd be feeling comfortable here. She...? She would be less so.

His outline appeared, coming down the hall, and when he opened the door Rebel rushed out to greet her.

'Hello, boy,' she said, ruffling his fur and making a big fuss of him before she looked up at Zach.

Wow. He looks amazing.

Dressed casually in blue jeans and a white fitted tee, he looked as if he'd stepped out of a jeans commercial or something. He was barefoot. *Barefoot!* And his clothes moulded his body with absolutely no thought or concern for how it might affect her.

She managed a weak smile as her heart rate accelerated, and with no other working thought inside her head she thrust the bottle towards him. 'To go with the chicken.'

He examined the bottle and smiled. 'Ah, my favourite! How did you know?'

His what?

Her mouth gaped open slightly as she recalled Stephen's slight smirk, and how he'd positioned himself behind the counter so that the only remaining bottle of white was the one that she'd picked out.

Zach's favourite.

'Erm… Stephen helped.'

He nodded. 'I bet he did. Come on in!'

Zach stepped back, allowing her passage, and her embarrassment lessened as curiosity to see what kind of place he lived in took over.

CHAPTER SEVEN

HANNAH LOOKED...AMAZING. There was no other word for it, really. She was wearing cute khaki dungarees and her hair was loose. At work, she usually wore a little bit of make-up. Eyeliner. Mascara. Stud earrings. But without make-up she looked even more beautiful. Fresh and appealing. *Au naturel.* It did something to him. Stirred his blood even more.

Once he'd closed the door behind her, he wasn't sure what to do. Take the wine into the kitchen? Make her a drink? But the words that came out were, 'Want a tour?'

She turned and swept her hair over her shoulder in a wave. 'Sure.'

So, his heart hammering in his chest so much he feared an arrhythmia, he led her into the lounge, glad he'd done a tidy-up before she got here. He wasn't an untidy person, but he'd wanted to make a good impression. He'd cut some flowers from the garden and they sat in a vase on the mantelpiece, and he'd switched on the corner lamps rather than the main light, for a little ambience.

He wondered what she'd make of his choice of art. A fondness for Art Deco posters was something he'd always had.

But did she notice any of those?

No.

'What is that?'

She'd gone over to his corner unit and lifted off the cuddly toy that sat on top.

He laughed. 'That's meant to be a baby haggis.'

She smiled. 'It's cute.'

Then she headed over to his bookshelf, and he watched her as she perused the titles. He had a mix of most things, but a particular fondness for historical fiction that had some sort of crime or mystery at its heart.

'You've read all of these?' she asked.

'Most of them.'

He showed her the kitchen, and then led her into the garden. He'd never been one to have green fingers. He could keep people alive, but plants had always been a problem. But then he'd got this garden, and his neighbours and the local garden centre had been so helpful that he'd finally been able to grow things successfully. He was pretty pleased with it.

'It's lovely, Zach. What are those?' She pointed at a small pot of flowers in various shades of pink, purple, yellow and white. They looked like large daisies.

'Mesembryanthemums,' he told her. 'They've started to close up for the night, but in the daytime they're at their best.'

She smiled and raised an eyebrow at his knowing their name. 'They're very pretty.'

Like you.

But he managed to refrain from letting that slip out.

His cottage wasn't very large. Only two bedrooms, though both of those were a decent size, and he'd maximised the space by having fitted wardrobes made to fit around the chimney breast. He showed her the guest room first, before his own room, and tried his hardest not to imagine what it might be like to lay her down upon the soft cover of his bed and see her hair splayed out over his pillows.

'I'd…er…better go and check on the pasta.'

She gave a nod, looking just as relieved as he to leave the bedroom space.

Downstairs, as he approached the kitchen, he turned to her. 'Can I get you a drink? Tea? Coffee? Something stronger?' He wiggled the wine bottle she'd brought.

'Wine would be great.'

'Perfect.' He grabbed two wine glasses and checked they were perfectly clean before undoing the screw cap and pouring them both a glass. He passed her one over.

'Thank you. So what are we having? Chicken…?'

'Chicken farfalle. My recipe calls for pancetta, but there wasn't any of that at the village shop, so we've got bacon that I've cut into small strips. And Dr Emery's grandfather gave me a whole bunch of asparagus the other week, so I'm adding some of that, too.'

'Sounds lovely. Can I help with anything?'

'Nope. Take a seat—it's nearly done.'

He busied himself for a while and that helped to calm his nerves. He so wanted this meal to be perfect. He didn't want the chicken to overcook and go dry, or for the pasta to be too soft, and he got so into what he was doing he almost forgot that she was behind him.

Almost.

But she was there. In his periphery. And he knew that she was watching him. He didn't normally get nervous like this and knew he had to calm down. This wasn't a date. This was just one colleague inviting another to dinner. That was all.

'How are things at Mrs Micklethwaite's?' he asked.

'Oh, you know… It's a bit like living at home

with your parents. There's a curfew. I can't have the television on in my room after ten o'clock at night and she doesn't like me to have visitors. No smoking. No drinking. And no longer than thirty minutes in the bathroom.'

He turned. 'You're kidding?'

'I wish I was.'

Zach laughed. 'Sounds like the care home I lived in on and off. The rules there were on laminated sheets stuck on the walls in every room. No chewing gum. No ball games after eight o'clock. Breakfast between six a.m. and eight a.m.'

'Wow. You must have been so happy when you got to leave and stay at a foster place?'

He shrugged. 'Sometimes. It depended if the foster parents were nice. Not all of them were. You could tell which ones were doing it for the money.'

'Did you speak to your foster father? The one going through chemo?'

She'd remembered. 'Yes. He was doing all right. A bit tired, but that's to be expected.'

Hannah nodded. 'When did you last see him?'

'I went up in February. Stayed for a weekend. I try and go a couple of times a year. How about you? When are you going to visit your family next?'

'Oh, you know… When I can get some time off from work. My boss can be a real bear.'

He turned and smiled. 'I hope you're talking about Lucy and not me.'

She laughed. 'Of course!'

He turned back to the stove, put butter and cream into a pan and let it bubble until it thickened. Then he tipped in the cooked chicken and asparagus. Then he drained the pasta and added it to the creamy chicken mix, stirring well. It was looking good. He was pleased with it. He ground some black pepper on it, sprinkled a little nutmeg and some parmesan he'd grated earlier.

'Here we go. Done.'

Zach filled two bowls. Topped each dish with a little of the crispy bacon and a few more shavings of parmesan and it was done.

'Voila. Bon appetit!'

'This looks amazing, Zach! You can cook!'

'Well, you don't know for sure yet. It might taste awful.'

'Let's find out.' She speared a piece of chicken and swirled some creamy pasta onto her fork, then tasted it.

He watched her face intently. He wanted her to love it. It was one of his favourite dishes to cook. It would mean something to him if she liked it.

Her eyes widened and she made an appreciative sound. 'Oh, my goodness, that's amazing!'

Zach beamed with delight and took a forkful himself. 'Thank you. I do my best. Much better than that sandwich you had planned.'

'You're telling me… Listen, if ever the doctor thing doesn't work out for you, you can fall back on being a chef.'

He laughed. 'I'll bear it in mind.'

She took a sip of her wine and looked at him consideringly. Curiously. 'What made you become a doctor? Did you always want to be one?'

'No. I dreamed of being an astronaut. I liked that idea of escaping earth for a while and floating around in space without a care in the world. And then I got to school and learned science, and realised that if you were in space you'd have plenty of things to worry about! But science— chemistry and biology—was a subject I really enjoyed at school. When I was fostered at Evelyn's I began to get interested in medicine, and it just kind of grew from there. What about you? What made you become a nurse?'

'Oh, gosh, I always wanted to be one—ever since I was a little girl. I can't tell you where it came from, but I do remember playing with my dolls, and instead of having tea parties with them I got them to attend clinics and hospital appointments instead. I was always bandaging them. I even had this one doll with soft arms, and I would get a sewing needle and thread and give her stitches!' She smiled at the memory.

He could imagine that. Her as a little girl, playing with her dolls like that. It was cute.

'I remember thinking that the human body was such an amazing thing. It could do so much, but it could break so easily. I really liked the idea of helping people. Does that sound clichéd?'

He shook his head. 'No. Not at all.'

'I did think about being a doctor. Once, anyway.'

'You did?'

She nodded. 'But it seemed like so many years of training and I was impatient. I wanted to get started. I wanted to be hands-on, and I felt that being a nurse would allow me to do that.'

'You could still be a doctor if you wanted to.'

'Oh, no, thanks! I love what I do. I can't imagine changing that.'

'Well, we're very lucky to have you.'

'Thanks.'

They both ate quietly for a minute or two.

'So…um…when do you think we ought to do our second practice date?' he asked, knowing he needed to break the silence, and also knowing that it would probably make her smile. He liked doing that. He liked seeing her smile.

'Gosh, I don't know. Um…when's good for you?'

'I don't know either. What's the etiquette for asking for a second date? How long do you wait? Where do you go?'

She blushed. 'I've been out of the dating world for so long I'm not sure my answers are applicable.'

'Well, we had a sort of late lunch last time. We're having dinner now—though this is just as friends and not as a date.'

She pointed her fork at him. 'Exactly.'

'So…something else, then? A film? Bowling? Ice skating?'

'Have you seen me try to skate?' she asked, going red in the face and laughing.

'No. But now you're making me think I want to.'

'Can *you* skate?'

'Never tried it, but it could be fun. Shall we?'

She shook her head. 'I'm not sure that's the best activity for me.' She looked down pointedly at her leg.

'You can do anything you want,' he said softly. 'Don't let it hold you back. The world is your oyster—prosthetic or not.'

She sipped her wine, considering his words. Maybe he was right? 'Sure! Why not?'

'Okay. Next weekend? Saturday? Say three o'clock? After your social group's walk? We can drive over to the nearest town. There's an ice rink there.'

'Zachary Fletcher… You do know we're both liable to come back with loads of bruises from falling over all the time?'

'But we'll have had fun—and isn't having fun together the point?'

She nodded. 'I guess it is.'

'Then it's a date.'

Zach and Rebel walked her home. It was such a lovely evening it seemed a shame to take the car.

'And, look…it's only nine forty-five, so you'll get back before your curfew,' he joked.

She smiled, wishing he wouldn't joke. Because he was just so cute, and just so perfect all the damned time! He was a doctor. He could cook. He loved animals. He cared for people. He smelt good. Looked good.

Did he taste as good?

I bet he does.

But she didn't want to think about that.

Zach deserved someone who could give him the whole of her heart. The whole of her being. And she simply didn't feel good enough for him. Besides, he was her work colleague and her boss, and that just had red flags all over it, didn't it?

She'd not been enough for Edward. Maybe she wasn't enough for anyone?

She'd begun to suspect lately that maybe her relationship problems with Edward had been there *before* the amputation, but she'd blamed everything on losing her leg. There'd certainly been a few arguments before that day at the theme park. He'd complained about the hours she spent at work. About how her patients seemed to come before him. Said that she always chose work over him.

'Do you think that we, as medics, always put work first?' she asked now, and looked at Zach, a slight frown between her brows.

'I don't know. Some of us, for sure. Being a medic can be a vocation. A calling. It's got to be. We certainly don't do it for the money or the long hours.' He smiled. 'Why do you ask?'

'It's something someone once said to me.'

'Your ex-fiancé?'

She nodded. 'Edward. We used to argue about it all the time.'

'What made you think about that?'

'What we're doing... The fake dating.'

'How so?'

'Well, we're trying to help each other out,

right? Make sure we say the right things on dates. Do the right things. And it just got me thinking… Edward always used to argue that I kept a piece of myself held back. Like he never got all of me.'

Self-preservation, she'd called it, but where had it come from? It wasn't as if her parents had a bad marriage. She'd grown up in a wonderful home and had very happy memories of her childhood.

But as she began to think about it a bit more, she remembered her mum's story. How she'd once been an incredible young woman. Intelligent. Worthy of going to university. She'd wanted to study astronomy. Had spent years staring at the stars through her father's telescope. But then she'd met and fallen in love with the man who had become her father, and her dreams, and the woman she was, had disappeared as soon as the ring had been slipped onto her finger. She'd become a housewife and a mother. And there was nothing wrong with either of those things, but she knew her mum had lost who she was. Had lost her passions and her dreams as she'd raised her children.

'Do you think that was true?' Zach sounded curious.

'I don't know. Maybe. But what if it was? What if all my relationships are doomed to failure because I hold a piece of myself back? What if we do all this fake dating and it doesn't make a blind bit of difference to me? What if I'm just faulty and can't be fixed?'

He turned to look at her. She could see him thinking and wondered what was running through his brain. Was he glad that he wasn't really dating her? If he'd wanted to date her then he would, but no, he was using her as practice for when the real love of his life came along.

'Have you considered the idea that you might have held a piece of yourself back from him because you knew deep down, subconsciously, that he wasn't the right man for you?'

Hannah stopped walking and turned to stare at him. No. She hadn't considered that. She'd been so focused on what might be wrong with *her* that she'd never considered there might be something wrong with Edward.

'Huh…'

'What?'

'I hadn't considered that.'

'So, let's think about it. Was there ever anything about this Edward that made you hesitate?'

'I don't like talking badly of people.'

'We're not. We're analysing. It's to help you. Consider it a fake date bonus.'

She nodded. 'Okay… Well, maybe he could be a little self-absorbed sometimes.'

'Okay. Good start. What else?'

'Selfish on occasion. Inconsiderate. A little rude to waiters.'

Zach smiled as he listened.

Her list began to grow, the more she thought about it. 'He wasn't keen on animals, and he told me that when we got married he'd never want a pet. Said they were too much work. Took up too much time. Made a mess. That kind of thing…'

'Deal-breaker right there, if you ask me.'

She laughed, but now she was on a roll. 'He'd eye up women when we passed them—even with me right there, holding his hand. He spent more time in front of the mirror than me, and before we'd leave the house he'd always ask me if his collar was straight. If his nostrils were clear. If his ears were clean. Honestly, he'd stand in front of me and expect me to check them! What was I? His mother? Why couldn't he look for himself, in that mirror he loved so much?'

Zach laughed along with her. 'There you go!'

'He wanted me to give up work when we had a child. I'd forgotten that. All those little things that he did that drove me up the wall. I was so focused on my recovery. On this image I had of myself getting to the church and getting out of my wheelchair and walking up the aisle. I was hoping to see an amazing smile light up his face. For him to cry with happiness... Oh, my God, Zach! I was in love with a fairy tale! Not the real-life version of us.'

She stopped walking as realisation hit. She couldn't believe it. Why hadn't she seen it before? Zach had helped her see with just a couple of simple questions and his support, telling her that it was okay to talk about it. That she wasn't doing anything wrong in bashing the 'brave fiancé' who had stood by her through her surgeries and amputation.

Because *he hadn't*. Not at all.

She looked at him in all seriousness. 'You're going to be an amazing guy for the right lady. When you find her. You do know that, don't you?' she said, wanting him to know it.

He looked at her strangely. 'And you'll be an amazing woman. When the right man comes along.'

At her lodgings, she decided not to drag out the whole goodbye thing. The last time had been awkward. The more she had stood there, the more she had wanted to do something. Give him a peck on the cheek, just as friends. But, terrified he might think it meant something more, she'd stopped herself—and then had lain awake for hours, reliving that moment and cringing.

So tonight she simply smiled, thanked him

for walking her home, placed her hand on his arm as a grateful gesture, then gave a brief wave and hurried inside.

Was that better than before?

Easier?

The answer was a resounding *no*.

CHAPTER EIGHT

PETER LAYMAN WAS an eighty-year-old gentleman who had come in for one of his monthly chats with Zach. He never came to talk about himself. Peter, despite his age, was still sturdy and strong, and the most that had ever been wrong with him was his Type Two diabetes, and he even seemed to have that nicely in control. No. He came to talk about something else.

Someone else.

'Hello, Peter!' Zach shook the man's hand as he came into his consulting room and bade him sit. 'How are you today?'

'Not bad, Zach. Not bad at all…'

He always said that. Zach sometimes thought the man's legs could be on fire and he'd still say, *Not bad. Not bad at all.*

'And how's Ellen?'

'Oh, you know how it is… The same, mostly.'

Ellen was Peter's wife of sixty years. At the age of seventy-six she'd been diagnosed with

Alzheimer's. They'd dealt with it alone for the first couple of years, but then Peter had begun to struggle with the behaviour and the moods, and after Ellen had nearly burnt the house down after leaving a chip pan unattended he had finally made the difficult decision to put his wife into a specialist care home.

It was a decision that Peter had struggled with immensely. He loved his wife, and felt it was his responsibility to look after her and do the best by her, and even though Zach had tried to present the idea of her going into a home as being best for her, as well as Peter, his guilt had weighed him down terribly.

'I went to see her yesterday,' he told Zach.

'How did that go?'

Peter shrugged. 'She didn't recognise me at first. That's always a blow. Sixty years with that woman at my side, and when I went into her room she just looked at me blankly and asked, *"Who are you?"* It's a hard thing, Zach. A very hard thing. She just doesn't see me.'

Zach nodded. He couldn't imagine loving someone for that long and then having that person not know who he was.

'Did she remember eventually? Did you tell her who you were?'

'Oh, yes. I got the photo album out. It took ten minutes, but then she said my name and everything was fine again. She even slipped her arm into mine and laid her head on my shoulder.' Peter smiled. 'That was nice.'

'Good. I'm pleased. How are her legs doing?' asked Zach. 'She had cellulitis, didn't she?'

'The doctors over there have been very good. Had her on antibiotics and it seems to be clearing up. Her skin's very dry, though, and the district nurse comes and has given the staff some cream to apply.'

'Good. It all sounds very positive. And how are *you* doing at home? Everything all right there? Any problems?'

'No. You know me… I can look after myself.'

'I know, but I have to ask. Are you lonely?'

'Sometimes. When you live with someone for that long you're used to just turning to them and making a comment about something, or asking a question. But when I turn around, even now, after all this time, I'm still surprised there's no one there.'

'Well, if you're interested, our nurse Hannah is running a group each Saturday for people on their own who want a little companionship. They meet here, and the local dog rescue centre brings over some of their dogs, and everyone walks together. It's very good and everyone has a wonderful time.'

'Ellen and I used to have a dog. Little white

toy poodle. Suzy, she was called. Nice little thing… What time does this group meet?'

'After lunch.' He reached for one of the flyers from his desk drawer and passed it over. 'All the details are there. Take a look. I think you might enjoy it.'

Peter nodded. 'I might give it a go. I got out of the habit of being with friends after Ellen got sick. And a few have since died, which you expect at our age. But this sounds interesting. I'll certainly give it a go. Thanks, Zach.'

'No problem. And if you ever need to talk—about anything—just call Reception and we'll fit you in, okay?'

Peter nodded and got to his feet. 'Same time next month?'

Zach smiled. 'Same time next month. Or any time.'

Peter shook his hand again and Zach walked him to the door, giving him a wave as he disappeared down the corridor.

He tried to imagine what it might be like to have been married for sixty years. What that would feel like. What a deep love it would have to be, to last that long… To build such a relationship, over time, only for it to slowly be eaten away by a disease that took that other person from you a little at a time, day by day.

Was that harder than losing them in an instant?

He didn't know.

On an impulse, he knocked on Hannah's door.

'Come in!'

He opened it and smiled to see that she didn't have a patient with her. 'Morning. How are you doing?'

'I'm good! How are you?'

'Great. I think I've got another person interested in your dog walking social group.'

'Oh?'

'Gentleman who's had to put his wife in a care home. Alzheimer's,' he explained.

'Oh, bless him. How is he?'

'He's managing. Just lonely, I think. He took a flyer—said he'd try it out. His name's Peter Layman. Just thought I'd better let you know that you might have one more this weekend.'

'Okay. I'll notify the dog rescue centre.'

'You still up for our ice skating?'

'I think so. You?'

'Yes. I did think about backing out for a brief moment. Because that's probably what I'd do if it was a real date.'

'You'd get cold feet about ice skating?' she said, and laughed nervously.

He nodded, smiling at her laughter.

He'd been an idiot to suggest ice-skating and

force her into it. But he'd meant what he'd said. She could do anything. He wanted to make her feel that she could.

'Well, if you put it like that... But I realise this is all about helping you find *The One*, so I'm going to be there.'

'It's meant to be helping you, too! Hey, I'm off to the bike shop tonight, to look for a decent mountain bike.'

'Want me to come along?' he asked. 'I said I would.'

'Oh! Well, that's very kind of you—if you're sure? I'd hate to keep taking up your time.'

'I don't mind. A promise is a promise.'

'Okay. I'm heading there straight after work in my car. It should only take half an hour or so.'

'Sounds perfect. I'll meet you after we've both seen our last patient.'

He left Hannah's room and then went out to deal with his little secret.

It felt strange to see Zach get into her car and smile at her before putting on his seatbelt. She appreciated him offering to come along and share his expertise on bikes, but she hadn't really expected him to do so. It was something he'd mentioned only casually—*'Oh, I'll help you, if you like.'* She'd never thought he actually would.

Edward had used to do that.

'I'll help you clear out that room. Don't want you throwing something important away.' Or, *'I can go shopping with you if you like.'*

But when the time came he'd always be too busy, or he would have made other plans, or he'd say he was too tired and he just wanted to relax and could they do it later?

'Which shop are we going to?' asked Zach.

'I thought the one in Cherringham.'

'Chrissie's Bike Shop?'

'That's the one.'

'I know it well. I got mine from there.'

She began to drive through Greenbeck, past the village green, over the Wishing Bridge, and then up the hill that would take them past the castle. Cherringham wasn't far. About a fifteen-minute drive. And Chrissie's Bike Shop sat in the centre of the small town, open that night until eight o'clock.

'Any news on Marvin?' she asked.

'Yeah, looks like he's developed quite an infection. They've put him on intravenous antibiotics to help get rid of it.'

'Poor guy. And your foster father? How's he doing since his chemo?'

'Yeah, good… He's had a couple of difficult days, but Evelyn said he was doing much better today.'

'That's good news. What are you doing with Rebel whilst you're at work?'

He laughed. 'Can you keep a secret?'

'Of course!'

'I brought him to work today. Settled him down in the old bike shelter behind the surgery, with a blanket, some toys and a bowl of water, and popped out in between patients to give him a quick cuddle and a toilet break.'

She laughed. '*That's* why I saw you out the back! For a minute there I thought I was going mad. But that *was* you in the woods?'

Zach grinned. 'Yes. Don't tell Lucy. You'll get me in trouble.'

'Hardly. You're the senior partner.'

'But Lucy's the practice manager and she used to be a nurse—you never mess with a nurse.'

'You'd better believe it!' She laughed with him, enjoying the fact that she was sharing his secret. 'Was Rebel all right?'

'He was fine! He was in the shade all day, and I took him food and snacks and toys...we had a walk. I think he enjoyed himself.'

'You love having a dog, don't you?' she asked softly.

He nodded. 'I do. I want Marvin to be better, but I'm really not looking forward to handing that dog back when he is.'

'I get that...'

They drove on in companionable silence for a little while as the traffic got busier heading into Cherringham. They got stuck behind a learner driver for a while, who stalled the vehicle at traffic lights, but they were in no rush so neither of them was bothered.

After finding a parking space in the town centre, they began their short walk to the bike shop.

'So, you say you're looking for a mountain bike?' said Zach.

'Yes. But I don't need anything with loads of gears and features. It's just to get me to work and back, and the occasional trail ride.'

'Have you got a helmet?'

'No.'

'Then you'll definitely need one of those. Safety first.'

'Good thinking.'

She pushed open the glass door to Chrissie's and they headed inside. Instantly they were surrounded by the smell of brand-new rubber and shiny, colourful bikes in all shapes and sizes. The young woman behind the counter looked up at them and asked if they needed any help.

'Not yet,' said Hannah. 'We're just browsing, thanks.'

'Well, I'm here if you need me.'

She beamed a smile, and Hannah couldn't

help but notice how the young woman kept sneaking looks at Zach. Did he notice things like that? He had to, right?

She noticed when guys looked at her. The appreciative smile. The second glance. The way their eyes would run up and down her body, as if she were some sort of commodity and they were trying to work out if she were worth pursuing.

She suspected that most would go running in the opposite direction after one look at her stump. Prosthetic legs were interesting, sure. And people admired you for having one in some ways. But not everyone found a missing leg to be physically attractive. She got that. So it was going to take a special kind of man who wouldn't be bothered by it. A man who would see beyond her physical disability. Beyond her missing limb. A man who found the woman behind it worth loving and much more important than anything physical that was missing.

Because she still felt whole. Wanted to believe that she *was* whole. It had taken her some time to feel that way and head out into the world like a brand-new person, but technically she was, and it had taken her time to get to know the new her.

'This one looks good.'

Zach was directing her attention to a silver-framed mountain bike. Looking it over, she kind of liked it. The style… The look…

He hefted it easily. 'It's lightweight. Want to try it?'

She grabbed hold of the handlebars and tried to swing her left leg over the crossbar. But her prosthetic foot didn't lift high enough and she stumbled, off-balance, and suddenly found herself caught in Zach's arms as he pulled her back to safety.

'Are you okay?' he whispered, his mouth by her ear.

Her heart thudded painfully in her chest, and even though her mouth was dry, and her body was going crazy at being in Zach's arms, she somehow managed a nod, her cheeks flaming red.

He seemed to be looking intensely into her eyes, and the feelings it created were crazy! His lips parted.

To kiss her?

'You need a lower crossbar,' he said, his voice strangely low.

He let go of her now that her balance was back. Of course. He was probably worried about her reaction to him holding her. He wasn't attracted to her in the least! They were here about bikes!

He walked over to another bike. Red, with

a silver and black streak of colour across the frame. It looked a lot easier to get on, and the seat didn't look as if it would slice her in two, either.

'Great.'

'Give it a try.'

Zach held the bike steady whilst she tried to get her leg over the frame and she did so easily. A label was hanging from the handlebars.

'"*Ten gears, lightweight aluminium frame, broad, deep-tread tyres, front suspension, disc braking system...*"' he read aloud. 'Sounds good to me.'

'What's the price?' she asked, still feeling slightly unsteady after what had just happened.

He turned the tag to show her.

'Not bad.'

'How does it feel?'

'Comfy. Surprisingly.'

'It's one of our most popular brands,' said the sale's assistant, who'd now come over, sensing a sale.

The name tag over her left breast said her name was Tayla, and she smiled at Zach once again.

'Could I test it out?' asked Hannah.

'Sure. We've got an area out at the back. Follow me.'

Tayla took hold of the bike, removed it from

its rack and began to wheel it towards the rear of the store. They passed through a door marked 'Staff Only', walked down a long corridor and then out through a fire exit, to where there was a large car park and, beside it, a small bike trail that went in a rough loop and included some small hillocks. No doubt for those who liked to perform jumps.

'Here you go.' Tayla removed the sales information from the handlebars and passed the bike to Hannah. 'Take it for a spin.'

A broad smile crept across Zach's face as Hannah set off down the track, wobbling slightly to begin with as she adjusted her balance and found the right place to situate her prosthetic foot on the pedal. Her hair streamed out behind her and he could hear her laughing as she went up and down the small humps on the track.

'You're doing great!' he called out, when she risked a quick glance at him and gave him a wave.

'It suits her,' said Tayla, glancing at him.

He had to agree. She looked amazing. But then again, she always did.

'Is she your girlfriend?'

The question pulled him out of his thoughts and he turned to look at the salesgirl. 'Er...no. She's a work colleague.'

'She's wearing a nurse's uniform. Are you a nurse, too?'

'I'm a doctor.'

'Oh? In a hospital?'

'No. A GP surgery.'

He whooped and clapped his hands in support as Hannah passed them once again.

'I wanted to be a nurse once.'

'Oh?' He gave the girl a quick smile, then turned back to watch Hannah.

'Didn't get the grades I needed for university.'

'That's a shame. You could always retake them, if that's what you really want to be.'

'Yeah, but it costs so much now, and I'm not sure I want that student debt hanging over my head.'

'It can be a worry.'

He didn't get to say any more. Hannah came to a stop in front of him, cheeks flushed red and an intense gleam of happiness in her smile.

'I love it! I'll take it!' she said, dismounting.

He couldn't help himself. He stepped forward and held his hands out, as if waiting for her to fall again, but Hannah frowned at him and, taking it as an admonishment, he stepped back.

'Oh, that's great!' said Tayla.

'Do you sell helmets?' she asked.

'We do.'

'I'll need one of those.'

They followed Tayla back into the shop and were shown to the helmet selection on the back wall.

'Wow, there's so many to choose from,' said Hannah.

'Which one do you fancy?' he asked.

'I don't mind, as long as it doesn't make me look silly.'

He wanted to say that it wasn't possible for her to look silly, but he held back, picking up a neon yellow and white one and placing it on her head, laughing as it pressed some of her hair down over her face.

Hannah laughed in response and adjusted the curtain of hair that had covered her face. 'What do you think?' She turned this way. Then that. Almost as if she was trying on a hat for a wedding. Then she looked in the small mirror at herself. 'Hmm… Not sure about the colour.'

Zach took the helmet off her and passed her a black and silver one, pressing it down onto her head and comically rapping on the top of it with his knuckles. 'How does that feel?'

'Actually, it feels all right.' Hannah adjusted the buckle under her chin and checked the fit and the look in the mirror. 'What do you think? I like it.'

She turned to him for his opinion. He knew

he was smiling. Broadly. Did he ever stop smiling when he was with her?

'Looks good.'

'Doesn't wash me out?'

'No.'

'I don't look awful?'

'No.' He wanted to tell her she looked beautiful, but didn't dare. He didn't want to come across as if he was interested in her.

'Wow... Save that charm for the practice dates.' She undid the clip and looked back in the mirror, so she didn't see the look that crossed his face.

She was more than beautiful. And she was one of the most courageous people he knew. Sure, he hadn't known her long, but even after all she'd been through she still had a wonderful outlook on life. After her accident she could have become bitter, or depressed, even angry. No one would have blamed her for that. But no. She'd fought hard to get back to a normal life. She still took care of others. She remained positive. And she was still looking for her happy ending.

She was beautiful inside and out. Losing a leg hadn't changed her. Being abandoned on the day of her wedding had been the thing to damage her, cause her to be afraid of being abandoned by anyone she had feelings for.

Something he understood all too well.

There'd been a long time as a boy when he'd not felt wanted. He'd never been adopted, though other children in the care home had been, and it had left him wondering what it was about him that made him unlovable? Was it because he was bigger than the other boys? More rough-and-tumble? Was it because he'd sometimes got into trouble at school? Or because he had dyslexia?

When he was fifteen, his first ever girlfriend had cheated on him. And during the upset Evelyn and her husband had fostered him. Maybe she'd taken pity on the young boy sitting in the corner with the sad eyes? She'd given him hope for a while, that maybe there wasn't anything wrong with him except for the fact that he wanted to belong. Because he'd always felt on the outside of everything.

Then his second girlfriend had also cheated on him. She'd said he came on too strong. Was too fast and too quick in telling her that he loved her and wanted to make all these plans. And maybe he had been. But he'd just been searching for a person to settle down with.

To make a family with.

To belong to.

So that finally he'd feel that he had a family of his own.

He'd gone to university determined to stay

single. To hold himself back...to remain separate. He'd learned that people he got close to only hurt him in the long run. He'd come top of his class, year after year, and although there'd been the odd date with other medical students during placements at the hospital there'd never been anything serious. He'd deliberately kept things casual. Fun. One night only. Until he came to Greenbeck.

In Greenbeck he'd worked hard to establish himself—and then he'd met Milly. Fun, energetic Milly, who understood what it was like to have patients and to put your work first, and he'd begun to believe that they shared a bond no one else could understand. He'd fallen for her hard. And he'd begun to believe that maybe he'd found the one.

Only to be wrong again.

'I'm going to take this one!' Hannah called out to Tayla.

'Great! I'll get everything rung up for you.'

Whilst they waited Hannah turned to him and smiled. 'Thanks for coming with me.'

'No problem.'

'We should meet up and go on a bike ride together sometime.'

He nodded. 'Sure! I'll look forward to it.'

Instantly his mind began to think of all the great places he could take her. Planning beautiful routes they could share. Maybe they could take a picnic and enjoy a day out? But he had to tell himself not to keep rushing ahead. He did this all the time—and she was not the right woman to rush ahead with. She was just his friend, nothing more. If she'd wanted to be with him she'd have shown him a sign, but she hadn't. They were each other's test subjects. Each other's guinea pigs. She did not want to go out with him!

So hold your horses. She's never going to be yours.

CHAPTER NINE

Mrs Janet Hancock hoisted herself up onto the examination bed and Hannah adjusted the back for her, so she was sitting up comfortably with a pillow supporting her lumbar region.

'I think it might be better… It feels better, anyway,' she said, as Hannah began to unwind the bandage that had been wrapped around her right foot by another member of the surgery team the last time she'd come in to have her diabetic ulcer checked.

'No pain at all?'

'No, nothing.'

People with diabetes could develop peripheral neuropathy, which meant that they lost sensation in their feet. No pain wasn't always good. Humans felt pain for a reason. It was a good thing. It told you to keep away from fire. It told you if you'd stepped on something prickly. Some diabetics caused damage to their feet because they couldn't feel that there was anything wrong, and the damage increased until it was too late to do anything about it.

After removing the bandage, Hannah carefully removed the gauze pad that had been used to cushion the underside of the heel bone, where there was normally a layer of fat. The pad was discoloured, and the wound had clearly oozed quite a bit. She tried not to show anything on her face when she saw the extent of the damage the ulcer had caused.

'This doesn't look good to me, I'm afraid, Mrs Hancock.'

'No? Oh, dear… How bad is it?'

Hannah could see bone—that was how bad it was. And the bone itself didn't look good either. If this infection had gone all the way into the bone and she'd got osteomyelitis…

'I think I'll need to get your GP to take a look at this as I'm not happy with it. Who's your doctor?'

'Dr Fletcher.'

'Okay. I'm just going to see if he's free. You stay there and don't move, all right?'

'All right…'

Hannah gave her a smile and then headed to Zach's room, knocking gently on the door.

'Come in!'

She opened the door and saw that he was alone.

'Just emailing a patient,' he told her. 'What's up?'

'Janet Hancock.'

'Yes?'

'Her ulcer's bad. I need you to take a look, but I'm pretty sure she needs to go to hospital.'

He sighed. 'Right. Okay... Two minutes and I'll be in.'

'Thanks, Zach.'

She headed back into her own room and began to wash out the wound, trying to get a clearer picture of what they were dealing with. The ulcer was sizable. At least two centimetres square at the staged edges. And Mrs Hancock's notes stated that she'd missed her last wound-check over two weeks ago.

Could they have done something more if she'd come in and not missed her appointment? Hannah had seen this kind of thing before. The patient couldn't feel anything wrong, so they ignored appointments and check-ups, but it was vital that they attended every one. Mrs Hancock had put her foot at risk. If the infection in the bone had gone too far, she could lose the foot—and Hannah knew how it felt to be told that sort of news. Knew how it felt to wake up from surgery and discover that there was a part of her missing for evermore. An empty space. The knowledge that you would never be the same again.

A knock on the door announced Zach's arrival and he came in. He said hello to Mrs Hancock and then had a good look at her foot. 'I think this needs to be looked at by a consultant, Janet,' he told her.

'You think so?'

'Yes.'

'You can't just give me some antibiotics and send me on my way?'

'No. Once the infection gets into the bone, it gets a lot more serious than a GP can deal with. And we want to be able to do everything we can to save your foot.'

'Save it? You think I might lose it?' Her voice filled with horror.

'Let's not go there just yet. Let's see what the consultant says. I'm going to give the hospital a call and then I'll contact you at home, to let you know what's happening. In the meantime, Hannah here will bandage you up and get you comfy again.'

'Right… Okay…'

'Try not to worry. I'll call you as soon as I've spoken to the hospital.'

'Thank you, Doctor.'

Zach gave her a nod and left the room, and Hannah began to rewrap Mrs Hancock's foot.

'That's scary…what he said. Do you really think I could lose my foot?' asked her patient.

'I don't know, Mrs Hancock. Let's hope not.'

'Don't know what I'd do! Woman of my age going through something like that.'

It was no fun for anyone of any age.

'Let's be positive. We have no idea if that's even going to happen. But from now on I want you to make me a firm promise.'

'What's that?'

'That you'll attend every single appointment given to you. Even if you feel okay. Even if everything feels fine. Can you do that for me?'

Mrs Hancock nodded. 'I can.'

'Good.'

'I'll be quick. Just a few words.'

Zach had called the staff to attention. They'd all been milling about in the main reception area, where Shelby's birthday lunch was being held. The reception desk itself was covered in various trays of food and drink, and helium balloons had been hung behind it.

All the staff, who'd spent ten minutes loading up their paper plates and mingling, settled down somewhat and waited for Zach to speak.

'First off, I just want to say how proud I am of

all of you. We work hard here as a team, looking after the people of Greenbeck, so when we get the opportunity I like us to celebrate each other. Celebrate the time, the care, the effort you put in to take care of our patients. Sometimes it can be difficult, when a person is alone, or in pain, or frightened, but I know that you guys can handle all of that. You reassure. You help. You care. And I couldn't ask for a better team. Shelby? It's your birthday! And even though you're at work...' he smiled '... I hope you have a fabulous day and that we see you bright and early tomorrow morning without a hangover.'

Everyone laughed good-naturedly.

'I'll try, but I can't promise,' Shelby said, raising her glass of non-alcoholic fizz.

He covered a few surgery updates. Read out a couple of feedback forms they'd had, praising members of staff. Then said, 'Okay, let's eat!'

Zach settled down in a seat next to Hannah. 'I've had an update on Mrs Hancock's foot,' he told her.

'You have?'

'It's definitely osteomyelitis. They're treating it with antibiotics at the hospital and she's going to have surgery for debridement and to remove an abscess. They're hoping that will be enough.'

'Fingers crossed, then.'

'Yes. She's upbeat, they say. I thought I might pop in and see her after her surgery.'

'Could I come along?'

He nodded. 'Sure. I think she'd like that.'

'I know how scary it can be. You know that the doctors are doing what they can to save your limb, but if an infection gets hold it can be touch and go.'

'I can only imagine...'

They watched as Shelby oohed and aahed over the cake that had been brought out.

'Who made that? Was it you, Gayle?' she asked, addressing one of the receptionists who often brought cakes in on a Monday for everyone.

'No, not me.'

'Then who?'

Daniel raised his hand. 'I made it. With help from Stacey.'

Shelby looked surprised. 'Who knew you had this in you?'

Zach noticed Daniel glance over at Stacey and wink at her. It was a friendly, conspiratorial wink. Then he caught Zach's eye.

He raised an eyebrow at Daniel as a rousing chorus of 'Happy Birthday' was sung. Afterwards, when Shelby cut into the cake and discovered that it was a rainbow cake, she made a strange squeak.

'A rainbow cake! Oh, wow, this is awesome!' And Shelby threw her arms around Daniel, surprising him, hugging him, before she turned and did the same to Stacey. 'You two are awesome!'

It made Zach happy to see his crew getting along so well. This was what it was all about. Family didn't always have to mean blood. And after his list of dating disasters he'd come to Greenbeck to find that he belonged somewhere. He belonged here.

'Daniel seems happy,' Hannah said.

'Yeah...' Zach smiled. 'I think Stacey and her young son Jack are giving him something to be happy about.'

'Really? Daniel and Stacey? I think that's great! They suit one another.'

'Well, I don't think it's official yet, and they think no one else has noticed, so let them keep that notion until it's announced for sure.'

Hannah nodded, and mimed a zipping motion across her lips.

'Are we still okay for ice skating?' he asked.

Hannah laughed. 'I guess so. I can't actually believe you've talked me into going.'

'It's important to not let anything hold you back—or so I've been led to believe.'

'You're right. I've heard that, too.'

Zach's plate was nearly empty. 'I'm going to load up on some more sausages and things. Sneak them out for Rebel. Cover for me?'

'Sure!'

He smiled a thank-you and got up to refill his plate with meaty treats. Then he successfully mimed getting a call on his mobile and headed off down the corridor, where the noise lessened. Soon he was at the fire exit and heading outside.

Rebel had been sleeping, but he woke at the sound of Zach's footsteps and got to his feet with a waggy tail and a wobbly butt.

'Hey, boy...'

He made a big fuss of the dog and lowered the plate for him to eat. He sat beside Rebel on the low wall, waiting for him to finish, and then they played for a short while. Rebel rolled onto his back for a belly-rub, which Zach happily gave him. They had another twenty minutes before afternoon surgery, so Zach decided to take him for a short walk.

He clipped on Rebel's lead, and when he stood noticed that there was someone at the window, watching.

It was Hannah, and she gave him a wave.

He waved back and headed off on his walk, his steps light and carefree, a broad smile upon his face.

***

Ice skating.

Hannah had her doubts about the whole enterprise.

She hadn't been ice skating since she was a little girl and she'd not been good then, with two legs. How on earth was she going to manage with a prosthetic? Would she even be able to get the prosthetic into a skate? The whole date could be a disaster before they'd even started!

But a practice date was a practice date, so she had to make the effort and not back out, because they'd promised one another and Zach was counting on her.

She was hoping not to develop any further feelings for him. Because Zach was great and she... Well, she was playing a dangerous game in continuing on with this charade.

The more time she spent with him, the more she found herself imagining what it might actually be like to be going out with Zachary Fletcher for real. How could she not? He was a great guy. But he didn't see her that way. Not in the way she would want him to. And even if he did, would she be brave enough to take that step? To put herself out there on the line? Knowing he could break her heart in two?

Because if it did all go wrong, then where would she be? Stuck in the surgery, working with him day by day, and everyone knowing they were exes. It would be as awkward as hell.

She'd spoken to Stacey and heard all about her last relationship with a fellow colleague which had gone wrong. The way Stacey had felt ousted from the practice because people took sides. That sounded horrific, and she couldn't imagine how Stacey must have felt.

If that were to happen to her, she had no doubt that people would take Zach's side, no matter how much they liked her. Zach was their boss. He was the senior partner and everybody loved him. He was kind and considerate and a great employer, and he really looked after his staff. They wouldn't risk losing any of that just to side with her. Would they? And then where would she be? Alone again. Rejected again. And she loved it here.

No. She had to tread carefully. To remember exactly why she was here with him at all. She was his practice buddy. His dry run. His guinea pig. She was the person he wanted to discover all his mistakes with, so that when his real true love came along he'd be perfect, and confident, and know that he could be the person she would need him to be without panicking about losing her. Without worrying that he'd say or do something stupid that would ruin it all.

He deserved that chance. He'd experienced

heartache, just like her. And Hannah was his marker. She was his dummy run. She was there for him to get things wrong with, so that she could point out what he needed to do to be right. She was the one who would bear the scars and the oopsie-daisies and the awkward moments, so that he could shine like the star he was when the right woman came along.

And when that happened she'd be left behind. To watch him fly.

With someone else.

She was his teacher, his instructor—nothing more. And she should teach herself distance. She would be good at that. It would make it easier when he sailed off into the sunset with another woman.

But what to wear today? She'd received a text from Zach two days ago saying that it was Disco Hour at the ice rink. Would everyone make an effort to dress up? She didn't want to stand out. It was going to be bad enough as it was, with her slipping and sliding everywhere and holding on to the barrier for dear life.

Throwing open her wardrobe, she looked at the possibilities. She did have an old pair of bright purple shorts that she'd owned since she was a teenager and never thrown away, but she didn't want her prosthetic leg on display so she dismissed those. Skirts and dresses were out of the question, too. She owned a rainbow-striped top. Would that do? Paired with some jeans?

If she remembered correctly, she had a pair that… She rummaged in the back of her wardrobe. Ah! Yes! There they were. Jeans with silver sequins along the leg seams. She'd bought them ages ago, thinking they were fun, but had hardly ever worn them after the accident. They were wide-legged, so should fit over her prosthetic easily.

Dressed, she looked in the mirror and smiled, turning this way, then that. She put her hair up into a high ponytail, put on some sparkly eye make-up and some large, dangly yin and yang earrings, and felt her look was complete—clashing and loud and out there.

It would have to do. Zach would no doubt laugh, but hadn't he said that dates were meant to be fun? If she was going to spend her time practising with him, then why shouldn't she have fun whilst she was doing it?

Downstairs, the doorbell went, and she heard the heavy footsteps of Mrs Micklethwaite as she went to answer the door.

'Er… Miss Gladstone? Dr Fletcher is here!'

Hannah's heart pounded, her stomach rolling in fear and excitement. If she went downstairs dressed like this and he was just standing there in jeans and a tee, she'd feel terribly embarrassed.

'I'll be down in one minute!'

Hannah sprayed a small mist of perfume onto her neck and fastened the high-top trainers she'd put on.

'What am I doing? What am I *doing*?' she muttered to herself as she gave her reflection one last look.

It wasn't too late to back out, was it? She could quickly change and go downstairs, tell him she'd changed her mind. That she didn't feel well, or something. Ice skating was going to be a risk. What if she made an absolute fool of herself? It would be hugely embarrassing!

But she wanted to spend more time with him. She *wanted* to.

And that urge overrode her fear completely.

Hannah headed downstairs, her nerves getting worse with every step, until she reached the bottom and saw him, still at the front door. Dr Zachary Fletcher. Dressed in a perfectly white suit with a black shirt underneath with wide lapels that almost reached the width of his shoulders. As soon as he saw her, he grinned and struck a pose. One hand on his hip, the other hand pointing up into the air.

Hannah instantly laughed. 'Oh, my goodness! That's perfect!'

'Think I'll be the only one there dressed like this?'

'Maybe!'

He smiled and looked her up and down. 'You look great.'

'Thanks.'

Zach gave her a small peck on the cheek, and then bent down to pick something up from the porch. It was a small bouquet.

'Tradition states a guy brings flowers.'

'They're beautiful. Let me put them in the kitchen. Do you want a tea or anything first?' she asked hopefully, wanting to put off arriving at the rink for as long as possible, so that Zach didn't get to experience her shame for a while.

'I'm good. Unless you want something?'

'No, I'm good too.' She smiled back at him, not sure what to say next.

Mrs Micklethwaite stood looking at both of them as if they were crazy. 'Maybe you ought to get going? I don't want the neighbours thinking I'm running some sort of retro lodging house.'

Hannah rolled her eyes good-naturedly. 'Okay. Thanks, Mrs Micklethwaite. See you later.'

'No later than ten,' she said, closing the door behind them with a solid finality.

'Your carriage awaits.' Zach indicated his car, parked at the end of the path.

On the back seat, she could see Rebel sticking his head out of the window. 'Rebel's coming, too?'

'Kind of. Next to the rink is a shopping centre with doggy daycare. I've booked him in there for a couple of hours. Didn't want to leave him home alone.'

'You're spoiling him!'

'Absolutely, I am. He loves being with other dogs, so I thought he'd enjoy it.'

Zach walked her to the car and opened up the passenger door for her. 'My lady.'

'Thank you, kind sir.'

He grinned, and once he'd made sure she was in safely closed the door and hurried round to the driver's seat.

'So, where did you find the outfit?' she asked. 'Or has it been lurking at the back of your wardrobe for years?'

Zach laughed. 'I hired it.'

'Really?'

'Of course! You think I had *this* lurking at the back of my wardrobe?'

'I had these,' she replied. 'Back home, we used to do a lot of dressing up. Halloween parties, Seventies dinner parties. Pirate and princess days. There was even a fairy hen party once.'

'Really?'

'Yep. In Amsterdam. I had to stand in Heathrow Airport dressed as a wood nymph for a whole hour before anyone else turned up.'

'Did you think they'd abandoned you?'

'I thought they were winding me up and they'd turn up in normal clothes and just the pink sash we were all supposed to be wearing.'

'But everyone turned up as fairies?'

'Yep.'

'I would have liked to see that.'

'I think I have a picture on my phone. Hold on…' She rummaged through the photo files on her mobile until she found the day in question. It held fond memories.

As he looked at the pictures she found herself looking at him. Studying him. He was just so…so…*perfect*.

'This was before your accident?'

'Yes.'

Of course, yes. Her fairy outfit had been short. He had to be looking at her legs, she thought. Wishing she were still the same now.

'You look amazing!'

She took the phone back and nodded. Of course he'd think that. She'd been whole then. Normal. Her life hadn't been destroyed by Edward, or a faulty roller coaster, or a stupid little bacterial microbe that had refused to submit to antibiotics. Clearly Zach thought she'd looked amazing then. She'd thought so too, and confidence had oozed out of her every pore. Back then she'd been young, pretty and carefree. With her whole life ahead of her. Possibilities galore. And the correct amount of limbs.

She wasn't like that now.

She was crippled. Not just by her body, but also by her emotions.

'Are you okay?' he asked.

Hannah forced a smile. 'Yes. I am. Come on! We don't want to be late for Disco Hour.'

Rebel put his head forward between the two seats and licked the side of Hannah's face. She turned and gave him a quick cuddle. Dogs always seemed to know when you needed cheering up. Perhaps she could do with an emotional support dog?

'Lie down, Rebel,' said Zach.

The dog lay down, and Zach started the engine and began the drive over to Cherringham.

'Let's hope we don't get stopped by a police officer. I'd hate to have to explain these clothes.'

Hannah smiled. 'That would be interesting! We could say we were time travellers from the past.'

'Yeah? And what have we come forward in time for?'

'To see what it's like? See if we're happy?'

'What if it was the other way round? What

would you be doing if we travelled into the past? Would you do anything different?'

'Personally?'

He nodded.

'Hmm... I don't think I'd have got on that roller coaster.'

'Then you'd be married. To Edward.'

Hannah frowned. He was right. She would be. How would that be? Knowing now that she'd always had doubts about him, she wondered if she would have gone through with it.

She'd kept on planning the wedding after the accident because it had been a positive goal, to keep her optimistic and her mind off her injury. Planning the wedding had kept her sane! But marriage to Edward? Would it have been rocky? Would it have failed before it had even begun?

'What would you change if you went back into the past?' she asked Zach.

He shrugged. 'I'm not sure. I guess I'd have liked to know my real mother. And who my father was. If she'd have kept me, my life might have been different.'

'Perhaps she couldn't. Perhaps she gave you up because she knew she wasn't in a good situation to look after you and she wanted you to have a chance in life.'

'True...'

'You might never have become a doctor, either. Might never have arrived in Greenbeck.'

'It's strange, isn't it? The *What would you go back and change?* question. It's tempting to think you would change your life for the better, but when you really examine it you discover just how much you'd lose from your present if you did.'

'Exactly. So, what are you grateful for right now? What's wonderful in the world of Dr Zachary Fletcher?'

He smiled. 'My foster parents. Greenbeck. Rebel. My work. You.'

She blushed. 'At least I'm in there somewhere! Although if this were a real date and she asked you that question I hope that you'd put her higher up the list.'

'Ah—noted! Anyway, I wasn't listing them in order of importance. I was doing it alphabetically.'

'Were you?' She thought for a minute, running his answers through her mind. 'Oh, yeah! Clever sod.'

'What about you, Hannah? What are *you* grateful for right now?'

'Hmm, let me see... *You!*' She laughed. 'Greenbeck. My family. My job. The freedom to just be me.'

'Disco Hour at the Cherringham Skating Rink?'

'Of course! It's given me the opportunity to see you dressed up like that.' She indicated his white flare-legged suit and wide seventies lapels. 'They're going to think we're weird when we take Rebel to the doggy day care first.'

Zach laughed. 'Maybe.'

They'd entered the outskirts of Cherringham. The skating rink was located in a large retail park that also contained a cinema and a bowling alley. Zach managed to find them a decent parking space, not too far away, and she became aware of the sideways looks they got as they walked Rebel to the Waggin' Wheels Doggy Daycare Centre.

'Disco Hour?' asked the young girl on Reception, smiling at their clothes.

'How did you know?' asked Zach.

'They have it every first Saturday of the month. You should see what some people wear! You two… You're not too crazy.'

'Glad to hear it. We'll collect him in an hour or two.'

'See you then.'

They walked out of the doggy day care centre and towards the skating rink.

'See? That wasn't too bad,' he said.

'No. I guess not. Oh, my gosh, look at that!'

Hannah pointed at a young man wearing a psychedelic jumpsuit heading into the skating rink. 'I guess we're not going to be the odd ones out, after all.'

He laughed and held the door open for her.

'Thank you.'

She smiled and they headed inside to buy tickets.

Her nerves were beginning to build. Getting dressed in weird clothes was one thing. Going skating was another. Would she be able to get the skate on over her prosthetic? she wondered again. If she couldn't this whole date would be ruined. If she knew anything about dating it was that ruining a date did not go down well, and they were trying to teach each other how to date well.

So she pasted on a smile and stood in the line with Zach as they waited to get their skates. Once acquired, they went over to the wooden benches to put them on.

Hannah spent ages loosening the laces, so Zach had his skates on well before her. She'd only got the right skate on, and was thinking about how best to tackle the left.

'Want some help?'

She looked at him, grateful that he understood. 'Please.'

And Zach got down on his knees, held the

skate in one hand and her prosthetic foot gently in the other, and slowly began to guide it in.

Was this what Cinderella had felt like? In that moment with Prince Charming was at her feet, sliding her dainty toes into the glass slipper? At least Cinderella had known her foot would fit!

'If it doesn't fit we can do something else,' she said, trying to sound reasonable and *Hey, I don't mind.*

He looked up at her, smiled. 'It'll fit. Trust me.'

His blue eyes sparkled and held such warmth. She wished she could feel his hands on her foot, her ankle, her lower leg. Feel the pressure of his fingertips against her skin. But all he was touching was plastic. Yet despite that she could still feel a rush. Could imagine what it would feel like. And when he slid her foot into the skate she felt a surge of happiness.

'You did it!'

'Of course!' He began to lace up the skate for her.

Hannah resisted the urge to reach out and run her fingers through his hair. To stroke the side of his face and say thank you. She wanted to—so much! Instead, she just beamed a smile at him when he was done, and he got to his feet and held his hands out to help her up.

She stood, expecting him to let go of her immediately, but he didn't.

'How does that feel?'

She knew he meant how did it feel to wear the skate on her prosthetic when she was only used to wearing a shoe? But her brain was registering what it felt like to be standing there holding on to his hands.

'It feels great.'

'Need me to hold your hand whilst we walk to the rink?'

'Er…yes, please,' she answered—simply because she wasn't ready to let go of his hand just yet.

And actually, as they began walking, she was glad she hadn't let go, because walking in ice skates was completely different from normal walking when you had a prosthetic.

She wobbled a little. Felt unsteady. Her hand clutched his arm tightly. She felt muscle. She felt solidity and strength and felt protected and safe.

'Okay?' He looked at her intensely. Caring etched deeply across his features.

'I'm good.'

They neared the entrance to the rink and Hannah looked out at the icy expanse, seeing all the other people dressed in disco outfits, whizzing here, there and everywhere. Everyone looked so capable—and she was not. Seventies music was playing, blaring out from the speakers, and there was a disco ball above the rink, splintering light in all directions.

Zach stepped out onto the ice first, getting the feel of it and holding on to the side with one hand as he helped her out on to the slippery surface.

She bit her bottom lip, expecting to fall on her bottom almost immediately, but Zach held her steady.

'I've got you. Don't be afraid.'

She nodded.

Zach didn't let go once. He held her left hand, whilst she held onto the barrier with her right, and slowly they began to skate forward.

It was halting, at first. She stumbled once, almost fell, but Zach steadied her, laughing, and she rebalanced herself and carried on. Soon she began to get swept up in the atmosphere as her confidence grew. The clothes, the music, the ice. But most of all in just being with Zach and holding his hand. It meant the world to her that he didn't let go, and she could tell, seeing how much easier he found it, that he could have easily skated on ahead.

Only he didn't.

He stayed by her side, making sure she was safe, and they were smiling and laughing and enjoying each other's company.

'Want to let go of the side?' he asked.

'I don't know…'

'Come on. Give it a go! I believe in you! I promise I won't let go.'

She nodded, and tentatively let go of the side, shrieking and wobbling and laughing so hard that she clutched at his arm and overbalanced. Her skates went out from under her and she grabbed onto him so hard she pulled them both down onto the ice.

Zach took the brunt, landing on his back, and she fell onto him.

They were both still laughing, but then she saw a look in his eyes that stopped her, and she stared into those blue depths and wondered, ever so briefly, ever so daringly…

'You know…if this were a real date, it would be the perfect moment to kiss.'

He gazed back at her. 'I think so too. Or else we'd awkwardly try and get back to our feet and pretend the moment had never happened.'

He was telling her what they should do, and he was right. Because it suddenly felt as if the moment had passed, and she became aware of people whizzing by them. She remembered that they were in a public rink, and probably causing an obstacle to other skaters, and reluctantly she got to her knees, grabbed the side barrier and hauled herself to her feet.

She held out a hand to help Zach up, and watched as he brushed ice crystals from his clothes.

'You okay?' he asked.

'Yeah.'

She smiled, feeling awkward, wishing she'd been brave enough to kiss him. Only she hadn't. Because this wasn't a real date. So she'd hesitated, frightened. What if she *had* kissed him? He'd clearly not wanted that, and then the whole day would have been awkward. Work would have been awkward!

No. I did the right thing. I think...

'You want to go it alone, or...?'

He proffered his hand again, but he couldn't meet her eyes, and she just knew, right there and then, that she had made him feel awkward with the way she must have looked at him. Suddenly she felt appalled and embarrassed. He'd obviously known that she'd thought of kissing him!

Shame flaming her cheeks, she held on to the barrier grimly and said, 'I think I'll try it on my own. You go on ahead. It's okay.'

He nodded. 'You're sure?'

'Yes. I just need to get my balance a bit better—you go and have fun.'

'Okay...'

She could tell he still had some reluctance at leaving her, but leave her he did.

Hannah gulped back tears as she watched him skate away. It was faltering, and he was clearly still trying to keep his balance, but he was doing it.

A thought entered her mind. She could take this moment of blessed relief, turn around and go home. It would be fine. She could get a bus, or a taxi. By the time he discovered she was gone it would be too late.

I'd never get this damned skate off!

And also she'd only be postponing the inevitable. There'd still be awkwardness at work. Trying to avoid each other. No, she had to stay. Had to hope that letting him move away and skate on his own would mean that by the time he caught up with her again the moment would have passed and they could pretend that it had never happened.

Besides, avoiding running away was the whole point of this practice dating endeavour!

Using the barrier, she pulled herself along, adjusting her balance, occasionally feeling steady enough to let go and test herself. It was exhausting, the amount of mental energy she was putting into her balance, concentrating on not falling. She barely noticed the music, or the other people. Didn't even have time to enjoy everyone else's costumes.

She stopped to rest and turned to see where

Zach was. She saw him instantly. On the far side of the rink, helping a young woman dressed in a silver sequinned dress get back to her feet. He was a gentleman like that. Good. Kind. Always trying to help.

The young woman had taken his hand, and even at this distance, Hannah could see her broad smile, the way she was laughing, the way she flicked her hair and kept laying her hand on Zach's arm as they laughed and joked about something. Hannah could see it was an obvious flirtation. This woman liked what she saw in him, that was for sure.

A surge of jealousy swept over her and, determined to ignore it—and what it meant—she continued to pull herself along the side of the rink. It was nothing to do with her. Zach could flirt with whomever he liked. It was quite clear that he didn't want to flirt with *her*.

She was so busy concentrating on what she was doing and making her first lap that she jumped when she felt a hand touch her arm.

Zach.

'Just me. How are you getting on? Any better?'

'A little. You were doing quite well.'

'Do you think so? I felt like a baby deer on ice.'

'No, you were doing brilliantly. I saw you helping that woman. Was she okay?'

'Och, she was fine.'

'She liked you. You should ask her out.'

There. She'd said it.

Because if she pushed him away and made him ask someone else out, then these ridiculous practice dates could stop and she could get some distance from him and stop all these ridiculous thoughts she kept having about him. Plus, hopefully, it would make him see that she hadn't meant it about kissing him when they'd fallen over. She'd just been speaking hypothetically—that was all.

Zach smiled and shook his head. 'I don't think so. Besides, I'm here with you, and I'm sure it's bad form to ask another woman out on a date when you're on one with someone else.'

'But you're not. Not really. This is a practice date. Why not see if you're ready for the real thing? Go and ask that woman out. I'm sure she'd say yes if you asked.'

He shook his head. 'No. I'm with you and... I'm not ready.'

'Well, at least go and get her number for when you are.'

'She's not my type,' he said firmly.

He sounded sure of himself. Certain. Determined. And his tone implied that he wanted her to end this conversation. She felt a little taken aback by it.

'Okay. Just thought I'd mention it. Fancy a break? Shall we get a drink?'

Suddenly Hannah wanted to get off the ice for a bit.

'Sure. I need a break.'

CHAPTER TEN

ZACH STOOD IN the café queue, waiting to buy a couple of hot chocolates, and saw Hannah had grabbed them a table. The ice rink's café sat alongside the rink itself, so the customers could still see everyone on the ice and watch people skating whilst they had a break themselves.

He'd needed to get off the ice. For a change of scene. A break. So many thoughts…so many feelings…had reared up in his mind over the last hour or so and he was feeling confused and worried.

It had begun way before the fall, to be honest. But with Hannah losing her balance, and him somehow catching her, overbalancing himself and pulling her down with him onto the ice… She'd knocked the wind out of him in more ways than one.

Something had happened in that brief moment when she'd lain half on top of him, staring into his eyes, and he'd looked into hers. There'd been an awareness. A wanting. If his life had been a romcom, that would have been the perfect moment to kiss her and change the course of the entire movie, and maybe his desire had been all too clear, because she'd said, *'You know...if this were a real date...it would be the perfect moment to kiss.'*

He'd even agreed! Out loud! Which had ruined everything. Because he'd seen the alarm in her beautiful eyes, the way they'd widened in surprise, and he'd realised all too quickly what a mistake he'd made. So he'd suggested an alternative idea instead.

'Or else we'd awkwardly try and get back on our feet and pretend the moment had never happened.'

And that was the face-saving option they'd gone with. Much to Hannah's relief, no doubt.

When she'd suggested he skate on his own, he'd agreed. Happily. Needing some space to get away and think. To calm down. To decide what to do.

Had he come up with any answers? No.

And then she'd said he ought to ask that woman out! The one he'd helped to her feet. Well! That was a clear indication from Hannah that she didn't want him to get any ideas about kissing her in the future! She was trying to get him to ask out another woman! Clearly she was embarrassed by him, and the sooner they stopped having these practice dates the better.

'Two hot chocolates, please,' he said.

'Marshmallows and whipped cream?'

He nodded and looked back. He could see that Hannah was looking away from him, towards the ice and the other skaters. See? She couldn't even look at him now. He'd been such a fool!

He'd been an idiot to think that maybe…just maybe…there could be something more with Hannah. He'd wanted to kiss her so much! But fear—his damned fear—had got in the way! He'd hesitated. And he couldn't help but think where they'd be right now if he'd just acted on impulse and done what he'd wanted to do.

I know where we'd be. Avoiding each other. After I'd apologised. She clearly doesn't want me.

She'd told him straight. *'This is a practice date… Go and ask that woman out…'*

She wouldn't have said that if she'd wanted to be with him, would she? She was clearly trying to politely steer him away from her. She was the only one of them thinking clearly. Thank goodness for her.

Zach paid for the two drinks and carried them over to the table on a tray. 'Here you go. Two hot chocolates with all the trimmings.'

'Oh, wow! These look great.' She smiled at

him, eyes sparkling, and then looked back at the rink again, watching the skaters. The ones who could twirl and pirouette and spin.

He took the opportunity to look at her and realised that no matter how much he wanted her he would never be able to have her. Hannah was simply doing him a favour. She was his practice date and nothing more. As he was for her. That was all. It was simple.

He needed to stop letting his thoughts and feelings run away with him, as they so often did in his secret yearning to find the one perfect woman he could create a family with. He often saw things that weren't there. It was a flaw. He needed to face it. Confront it. And wasn't that the whole point of these practice dates? Perhaps if he showed her that he was learning from them, and changing, they could end these things and he wouldn't have to torture himself by spending time with her?

'So, what did you think to your first skating experience?' he asked, trying to get her to engage with him at the table.

She turned to him. 'It was…interesting. Harder than it looks on TV.'

'Definitely. It seems to hurt more when you fall as an adult.'

Hannah nodded, taking a small sip of her hot chocolate. It left a little line of cream along her top lip, and he didn't know whether to reach out and wipe it away with his thumb, or just mention it.

'You have a...erm...'

He pointed at his own mouth and she quickly grabbed a napkin and dabbed at her face.

'Thanks.' She blushed.

'I'm sorry if I pulled you down with me,' he said. 'I was trying to stop you from falling, but I overbalanced. I just wanted to say sorry for that.'

'It's fine.'

'No, it wasn't. It led to...' He swallowed hard as he saw fear and uncertainty wash over her features. 'To you falling on me. And there was a moment there that... Well, I guess we both know it was awkward, right?'

Hannah looked down at the floor, cheeks flushing with a heat that he knew was nothing to do with the temperature of her drink.

'You thought I wanted to kiss you,' he said. 'I know you did. You said so yourself that that would have been the perfect moment. I'll admit the thought did cross my mind, but...it would have been the wrong thing to do—obviously. I don't know why I even thought it.' He smiled ruefully. 'So, I'm sorry. It was a learning experience, though! Honestly. And I want to thank you for that.'

'Oh! Well… I'm glad I'm helping, then.'
She gave him a brief smile that left her face as
quickly as it came. 'You've helped me and I've
helped you—and that's what this is all about,
huh?'

'Absolutely.'

'Maybe we're cured?'

He managed a small laugh. 'Maybe.'

'Perhaps we should try dating other people
properly now? Now that we've had our eyes
opened by each other?'

Zach nodded slowly, not liking the idea one
bit. But maybe she was right? Maybe they had
become too close through this process?

'I guess we should…'

They both sipped their drinks quietly.

Hannah picked up her teaspoon and began
to take small mouthfuls of cream and marsh-
mallow. Eventually she said, 'You know… I'm
kind of tired. Would you mind if we went home
soon?'

'Not at all. Shall we finish these, then go?'

'That'd be great. Thanks.'

She'd not been able to wait to get home. After
leaving the rink they'd collected Rebel, who'd
been overjoyed to see them, licking them both
profusely before he could be calmed down
enough to get his lead clipped back onto his

collar, and then they'd got back in the car for the drive back to Greenbeck.

Thank heavens for the radio, playing softly in the background, otherwise the journey might have been made in utter silence.

Now, as Zach pulled up outside Mrs Mickelthwaite's, she pasted on a huge smile and gushed about what a wonderful time she'd had, thanking him.

She was about to get out of the car when Zach had said, 'Hannah, please wait.'

She frowned, looking at him, wondering what he was going to say. Hopefully something that would clear up this mess that had come since their fall at the rink. Would he say something about the near-kiss? Something that would make seeing each other at work easy.

But he looked tongue-tied. Was frowning slightly as if he was searching for the right words. And then he looked at her, sighed, and reached for her and pulled her lips to his in a sudden kiss.

She almost gasped, she was so taken by surprise. But her shock soon gave way to enjoyment as she sank into everything he was making her feel.

He was a fine kisser. A very good kisser. His bristles tickling her face, his hand in her hair at the nape of her neck...

She needed to breathe. Didn't want to breathe. Didn't want to stop this. Who needed air? Not her.

And as the kiss deepened she felt her body come alive. Every nerve-ending was firing into life, her body demanding to be touched, or caressed or teased.

His kiss was everything she'd imagined it could be and more. Gentle. Passionate. Expert. Delightful. Arousing.

Goodness me, this man is a gift!

And then he broke away. Met her gaze. Looked at her uncertainly, not sure of her response. He let go of her, sat back in his seat.

She stared at him, her mouth still open, still breathless. She wasn't sure what she was supposed to do now. Or say!

'If that had been a real date, then that's how it should have ended. Just so you know,' he said.

She nodded and got out of the car.

Hannah got to work early on Monday, locked up her new bike in the bike shed, and was very much relieved to see that Zach's car wasn't there yet. In her room, she hung up her jacket and bag on the back of the door and began to prep for the day.

Her first patient was a stitch removal. She didn't normally deal with that—usually the

HCA took care of it—but there was a note on the system to say that everyone else was fully booked and they'd needed to place this patient with Hannah. Lucy, the practice manager, had approved it, and Hannah was glad to do it and have something practical to focus on first thing.

Normally when she arrived for her working day she would spend some time in the staff-room. Get the kettle boiled, make everyone drinks and socialise for a bit. But not today. Any time she spent with Zach was going to be awkward, and she didn't want other people to notice it and start commenting about it. Or even gossiping. Not that she thought that anyone would do so maliciously, but it happened even in the nicest of places.

She wanted to forget their last practice date, but she couldn't get the image of his face out of her mind. She'd practically been lying on top of him. Their faces inches away from each other. There'd been an awareness in each other's eyes. That look of uncertainty. *Temptation.* That had been the most difficult thing. Had he seen the temptation within her?

And then that kiss in the car. That had been… out of this world! But it hadn't been real. He'd said, *'If this was a real date, then that's how it should have ended…'* And he was right. They hadn't been on a real date. But a man who could kiss like that...

Her computer beeped to let her know that her first patient had arrived so she called them in.

Mr Souness ambled into the room and gave her a smile. 'Morning, Nurse.'

'Good morning, Mr Souness! How are you today?'

'Not bad...not bad. Carrying on, as you do.'

She smiled. 'And how's the leg been?'

'Fine! Nothing to report—and I hope you don't tell me anything otherwise once you've seen it.'

'Shall we get you on the bed?'

He nodded and clambered up, and she helped him lift his legs. The injury was on his lower leg, and it stated on the system that the wound was near the ankle, so she didn't need him to remove his trousers.

'Let's take a look, then. Remind me how you did this?' she asked, as she began to unwind the bandage.

'Chasing after a young woman,' he said, and chuckled.

'Really?'

'Well, kind of.' He blushed. 'I met someone. Someone I hadn't seen for over fifty years. But she was my first love—and you never forget your first, do you?'

'That's what they say,' she said, knowing that she'd never forget Edward, but maybe for entirely different reasons than him being her first true relationship. His abandoning her at the altar would be the primary reason.

'I was on a cruise to the Norwegian fjords. One of those singles cruises. I wasn't looking for love, just friendship. Companionship, you know?'

She nodded as she removed the last of the bandaging and began to take off the gauze pad to expose the seven stitches that lay in a line just above his ankle.

'And there was Stella. We knew each other at school when we first went out, and I'd never forgotten her. But life got in the way, and we both got married to other people, and then we both lost our spouses and ended up on the same cruise. Oh, it was so good to reconnect! To speak to someone who I felt really got me, you know?'

Hannah examined the wound and found it to be perfectly healed. No sign of redness or weeping or infection. The stitches were good to come out.

'We had nine wonderful days together, and then, when we docked in Southampton, I was trying to catch up with her as we headed back onto dry land. I tripped and fell and caught my leg on another person's luggage.'

'Causing this wound?'

He nodded. 'Apparently I've got friable skin—whatever that means.'

She smiled. 'It means your skin easily tears or breaks down. Or it can bleed if gently manipulated.'

'Oh. Well, that sounds about right. Poor Stella felt so guilty for rushing ahead, but she was so keen to see her grandchildren, who were waiting to pick her up from the ship, she couldn't help but go faster than me.'

'Well, it all looks fine to me, Mr Souness. I can take these stitches out, if you're happy for me to go ahead? It shouldn't hurt.'

'Please do.'

She grabbed the knot of the first stitch with her tweezers and used the stitch cutter to cut it and pull it free. 'So, it's been about twelve days since your accident. How are you and Stella now?'

'We're okay… I think. You'd think it'd be straightforward at our age. That we'd both know what we want. And we do. But trying to combine our lives when we've both got so much baggage between us is proving a little tricky, if I'm honest.'

'That's understandable.'

'And it's real now. On the boat, it was a different world. Like reality had been suspended. We could pretend we were fine and ignore all the little niggles.'

'I can understand that.'

It was similar to her pretending to date Zach. Reality, who they really were, didn't count. They could both be someone else before reality came back to bite them both on the butt.

'I do love Stella, and perhaps I always have, but I'm different now. I've been through things. Losing my wife was one of the most horrific life events I've ever had to get through. On the boat, it was fun. It was casual. It was good to get to know her again. But if we carry on seeing each other...' His voice trailed off.

'You don't want to get close in case you lose her, too?'

He nodded. 'Yeah... We're not young whippersnappers, either of us. And she's had cancer once. Breast cancer, she said. It's terrifying, to be honest. And look at me. I've already got my first wound.' He pointed at his leg and chuckled to lighten the moment.

Hannah wasn't sure what to say to him. Was she even qualified to advise about love? Was anyone?

'I guess you've got to take it day by day,' she told him. 'Don't rush into anything until you're absolutely sure. I'm sure she feels the same way, too, and has the same hesitations.'

'Happen you may be right.'

She removed the last stitch, very happy with the procedure. 'There you go. All seven stitches. You should be fine going about your daily routine, but be careful and don't knock this ankle, okay? You don't want to open it up again.'

Mr Souness smiled and nodded. 'Thank you, Nurse. And thank you for listening.'

'My pleasure. And I hope that you and Stella get to find the happiness you both deserve.'

'Thanks, love. You take care.'

'I will.'

She helped him off the couch and he ambled back out of the room. She quickly cleaned the bed and her instrument trolley, wiping everything down, and then sat at her computer, inputting notes into the patient's record. She liked Mr Souness. He seemed a nice chap. And it was obvious from him that, no matter your age, relationships weren't easy.

You'd hope that by the time you reached your sixties or your seventies you'd have everything worked out, but maybe love was never meant to be simple? Maybe something worth having had to be fought for? Had to be difficult? Otherwise you wouldn't cherish it as much? If love was easily attainable, maybe it would hold less value?

Her next patient had a urinary infection, for which she prescribed some nitrofurantoin. And after that she saw a child with bronchitis. Then came a woman with tonsillitis and tonsil stones.

Hannah had quite a productive morning, whizzing through her appointments steadily, until she reached eleven-fifteen, her morning break time, and she realised that she was terribly thirsty. She'd had nothing to drink since seven that morning, and she'd been working hard and talking a lot.

It was essential to chat to her patients in order to make them feel at ease, but she also wanted to get to know them better. They were hopefully going to be her patients for a long time, and she wanted a good relationship with them all.

She had no water in her bag, and she knew she'd have to get herself something from the staffroom. But all the clinical staff at Greenbeck had their morning break at eleven-fifteen, and she was worried that Zach would be in there. Pulling up the patient lists, she saw that Zach hadn't yet ticked off his last patient, so hopefully he was still in his room treating him. Doctors often ran late, as some patient consultations took longer than the allocated ten minutes.

So she got up and headed to the staffroom,

walking quickly to the small kitchenette and grabbing herself a glass so she could get some water. Ideally she wanted tea, but that would mean waiting for the kettle to boil and Zach could come in at any time.

Hannah filled her glass and smiled at Daniel as he came into the staffroom, saying good morning, and then headed back to her room. Just as she was passing Zach's door it opened. A patient came out, gave her a smile, and then there he was, looking at her, a hesitant smile on his face.

'Good morning.'

'Morning.'

Would it be rude to go straight to her room? She managed a quick smile and held up her drink, as if to say, *Must get on. Busy. Sorry...* And then she headed to her room, closing the door behind her with relief.

She'd just sat at her desk with a heavy sigh when there was a knock at her door.

Her heart jumped in her chest. 'Yes?'

'Can I come in?'

Zach.

If she said yes, they'd be alone in the room—and goodness only knew what he wanted to say! But if she said no...she'd feel awful. And she'd be making everything worse! Better to face it and get it over and done with.

'Sure—come on in.'

He opened the door, looking stunning, as always, in dark trousers and a pale blue shirt that had a faint white check patterning. It brought out the blue of his startlingly gorgeous eyes. His thick dark hair looked slightly mussed, as if he'd been running his fingers through it recently, and she couldn't help but think what it would be like to run her own fingers through it…

'What can I do for you?' she asked.

'I need us to be as we were before.'

Heart. Pounding. Maddeningly.

'I'm sorry?' she said, as if she didn't quite understand him.

'Things are different…since the ice rink incident. And the car. I'm sorry. I should never have…' His voice trailed off and he swallowed hard. 'What happened in the car…we were still pretending, right? And you're my friend, and I don't want to feel like we need to avoid each other. Not here. I won't allow it. This should be our safe space. Our *comfortable* space. And I want back the bubbly, happy Hannah that I first met. Tip-top Hannah.'

He smiled.

She smiled, too. Remembering that first day. That first embarrassing day when she'd thought all was lost, when actually it hadn't been. He was right. They shouldn't have to avoid each other. Not here or anywhere. They were grown-ups, for crying out loud. No one had died. Nothing terrible had happened. They'd just kissed. And, even though that kiss had been the most spectacular thing she had ever experienced, it had been just pretend.

Hannah nodded. 'You're right.'

'We're good?'

'We're good.' She smiled at him, and he sank into a chair opposite her.

'Great. I'm glad to hear it. I missed being able to talk to you this morning.'

'I missed that, too. And my morning cup of tea!' She jiggled her almost empty glass of water in front of him.

He laughed. 'Well, we can't have that. Want me to go and make you one?'

He was so kind.

'I'll come with you.'

And they headed back to the staffroom together.

Zach was thrilled that they were on talking terms again. It wasn't exactly as it had been before, but it was close to it. And he knew that with a little more time it would return to normality. They just had to wait for the awkwardness to get out of the way first.

To accelerate that process, he'd asked Hannah

if she wanted to join him on a trail ride, using her new bike. She'd agreed, after a brief hesitation, and he was now waiting for her to arrive.

He'd initially wanted to meet her at her house and cycle from there, but he'd held back from suggesting that, not wanting it to seem like a date. This was just two friends…meeting up to enjoy a little bit of exercise and then going their separate ways.

So he'd suggested they meet at the village green. By the bench next to the duck pond. It seemed a nice, neutral spot, and now he'd arrived he could see that the team responsible for organising the village fete had begun their decorating. He could see lines of bunting going up, and from where he stood he could also see Walter and Pauline, the two stalwarts of any village organisational team, standing at the bottom of a ladder, issuing suggestions to a young man at the top of it, who was trying to attach a banner that went over the main road into and out of Greenbeck.

Pauline held a clipboard, whilst Walter was giving instructions. 'Higher. Lower. To the left. No. Not that left. My left.'

He smiled, and then his gaze was caught on a movement to his right and he saw Hannah pedalling towards him, a big smile on her face as she gave him a little wave.

Zach waved back and waited for her to come to a halt in front of him. It was a Thursday evening and thankfully they still had plenty of daylight hours left.

'Hey. Looking good! How are you enjoying it?' he asked, indicating the bike.

'Great! I've had to adjust the seat position, but it feels much better now.'

'Aye, you'll have to tweak a lot of things at first, until you get used to it. What sort of ride do you fancy? A road ride? Or a trail? There's a good one through the woods that's not too much uphill.'

He couldn't help but notice how great she looked. Normally he was used to seeing her in her nurse's uniform, but now she wore a tight cycling top and long sports leggings that covered her prosthetic down to her mid-calf. He tried not to stare. The clothing accentuated her curves, which he knew he was already drawn to. The figure-hugging sportswear was doing him no favours.

'Trail sounds good. Why don't you lead and I'll follow?'

'Okay.'

He pulled on his helmet, fastening it beneath his chin, and mounted his bike. It would be better for him to lead. Then he wouldn't have to worry about how distracted he'd get if he had to follow behind her.

Setting off, he glanced behind him to make sure she was matching his speed, and then steered them towards the woods behind the surgery.

At this time of day the heat had begun to wane, but sunlight still glinted through the gaps in the canopy above. It was perfect. His nose filled with the aroma of earth and leaves and pine cones.

The beginning of the trail was slightly uphill, and he could feel his heart pumping hard to get up the slight incline before they took the path that would level out and lead them along the valley in which Greenbeck nestled.

'You okay?' he called.

'I'm doing great!' she called back, and he grinned, steering off to the left slightly as the trail widened, so Hannah could catch up and ride alongside him.

He gave her a smile, and she smiled back, and in that moment he thought she looked beautiful. Her brown curls were escaping from beneath her helmet. She looked happy. Sunlight shining down on her face. Sparkling eyes. A truly gorgeous and wonderful woman. He felt lucky to be with her. To have her by his side. He hoped it could be like this always.

Tearing his eyes away, he glanced forward, avoiding a tree root that was quite prominent, steering around it and then continuing on.

'Isn't this great?' she asked.

'It is. There's nothing like it.'

'Where does this trail take us?'

'It takes us parallel to Greenbeck and then further out into the valley...past a few farms. We can do a giant loop—it's about fifteen kilometres in total. Is that okay?'

'As long as we can stop somewhere to rest!'

He nodded. 'There's a pub around the halfway mark. The White Rabbit.'

'Sounds perfect.'

They continued their ride together. Talking. Laughing. Just enjoying being in each other's company.

After about three kilometres the woods opened up into a green valley and fields, and before they knew it they'd come across a farm filled with alpacas. Hannah asked if they could stop to take a look.

They pulled to a halt and parked their bikes against a fence, and Zach watched as Hannah held out her hand to a white alpaca that was standing by the field's edge, curious about its new visitors.

'Oh, my gosh, aren't they cute?'

He laughed. 'They are.'

He pulled at some long grass growing on their side of the fence, passed some to Hannah, and she fed the alpacas, chuckling at the way they chewed, how their ears flicked back and forth, and how they kept a curious eye on both of them.

'I think I read somewhere that alpacas can be used to protect other farm animals. They keep foxes away from chickens and ducks—that kind of thing.'

'Really? That's cool.'

She reached out to stroke a chocolate-brown one that had joined them at the fencing. He saw it was missing a leg.

'Oh, Zach…look!' She pointed.

But the alpaca was doing just fine. In fact, it was bigger than the others, and ambled about the field without any difficulties. He watched Hannah as she gazed at it, marvelling, and then she let out a huge smile.

'It doesn't matter to the alpaca, does it?'

'No.'

'It just carries on. Doesn't let it hold it back. In fact, it looks like it's the one in charge!'

She was right. The bigger alpaca seemed to be herding the others away from the fence, as if it were telling the smaller ones to be careful.

'It's what you do with them that counts…' she mumbled.

'Sorry?'

She looked at him. 'My dad. After my accident, he told me there's a saying. *It's not the cards you're dealt that matter—it's what you do with them that counts.*'

Zach nodded. 'Sounds like a wise man.'

'He is.' She paused. 'Zach, have I been letting this hold me back?' She knocked on her left thigh with her knuckles.

'No. I don't think so.'

'But I have, though! I might not show it, but I'm worrying about my leg all the time! I know a part of me is missing and I let it affect me. This alpaca doesn't! Those hundreds of cute videos you see of three-legged dogs and cats don't either! They're still full of joy…they still live their lives to the fullest…and yet I've allowed this thing that happened to me to mark me out in some way, as if I'm different. I'm not. I'm differently abled, and that's all. But I've allowed it to cripple me emotionally! I've held back from things because I'm scared all the time!'

'Hey…' He touched her arm, then let go. 'You're not scared. You're the bravest person I know.'

'You're just saying that because you have to. Because you're my friend and you like me.'

'No, I'm saying it because it's true. Because I mean it. Do you know how many people would still be suffering from depression because of an accident like yours? How many who'd be bitter? Or angry? And yet you're always smiling. Always determined to find the silver lining in everything. And you help other people feel brave. Look at how you spoke to Jack, Stacey's son. Look at how you create support groups for people and take an interest in their lives and try to make them better. Look at how you've tried to help *me*! You're a gift to this world, Hannah, and don't you forget it!'

He'd not meant to get angry, or passionate, but he couldn't bear to see her second-guess herself like this. To see herself as weak. Because she wasn't. She never could be. She'd been through so much, and if this was how she'd come out the other side then he could only hope he'd have been half as brave as her.

She stared at him. Shocked. He saw her gaze drop to his mouth and then she turned away, looking back at the now retreating alpacas.

'Thank you.'

He let out a breath. 'You're welcome.'

He wasn't sure where they went from here. Why was he always ricocheting about in his emotions when he was with her? Moments of calm. Moments of happiness. Then moments of terror and surprise and desperate frantic panicking and then relief again. Calm again. Certainty. Happiness.

He realised he couldn't bear to see her question herself. Couldn't bear to see her sad. Or regretful. She was beautiful. Inside and out. Her heart was kind and thoughtful and generous. She made him smile all the time. Made him laugh. Made him feel content. When he was with her, he felt...complete.

His heart pounded at the realisation.

'We should make a move,' he said quickly.

She nodded and they got back on their bikes and continued to cycle down the trail.

He led the way once again. But instead of being able to enjoy the countryside, the green fields, the tidy little farmhouses tucked away into the hills, the flowers and the occasional rabbit they saw dart across their trail, his mind was focused on Hannah and what she meant to him.

She meant a very great deal, and he knew he would do whatever was in his power to make sure she was happy. Even if it was at great cost to himself.

The rest of the week had been uneventful. Hannah felt that she and Zach were returning to normal, which was great, because she knew that things had got awkward between them after the ice skating and that kiss. The bike ride had helped—spending time together with no expectations other than cycling and enjoying being out and about in the evening air.

And then there'd been her small revelation when she'd seen that three-legged alpaca. It had given her a new outlook. A change of perspective. And she'd decided, there and then, that she was not going to let her lost leg hold her back. If she wanted something, then she'd go for it. If she met someone she liked, she'd ask him out. And if *he* had a problem with her leg, then that was going to be *his* problem. Not hers.

It had lifted a weight from her shoulders. Put a spring in her step. Something she felt had been missing for some time.

'I just wanted to say how much I've been enjoying this group, Hannah,' said Peter, the patient that Zach had introduced to her dog-walking group, whose wife was in a care home facility with Alzheimer's.

'Oh, I'm glad,' she replied.

'I got to chatting with Alma and Geoff the other week, and it was so nice to have a proper conversation again. It's funny how you miss simple things like that when you're alone.'

She nodded.

'Geoff told me about how he goes fishing on a Sunday, over at Cherringham Lake. And, by golly, I hadn't been fishing since I was a boy.

So he's offered to take me and we're going to make it a regular thing.'

'That's fantastic! I'm so pleased! I hoped this group would help people make new friends and connections.'

'And what about yourself?' asked Peter.

Hannah frowned, amused. 'What do you mean?'

'Well, surely you don't want to hang around with us old people each weekend!' He smiled. 'You must have friends, or someone special to share your time with?'

'I'm more than happy to spend time with you, Peter. Age doesn't come into it if you're with people you like.'

He smiled back at her. 'Ooh, here we go—the boss is coming. Look lively!'

She looked up and saw Zach approaching with Rebel. The sun was behind him and he looked gorgeous in blue jeans and a white shirt, his sun-tanned skin revealing dark chest hair at his throat.

'Zach! I wasn't expecting to see you today.'

'Well, Rebel seemed restless, and it looks like Marvin will be out of hospital tomorrow, so I thought I'd bring him out for one last big walk. I'm going to miss him.'

Hannah noticed that Peter had hung back to walk with the rest of the group, perhaps so that she and Zach could talk together in private. 'You'll still get to see him,' she said. 'He'll be right next door.'

'I know, but when you've developed a bond it's not the same thing, is it?'

'I guess not...'

She understood. She'd got used to seeing Zach with Rebel, too, and couldn't imagine seeing him without him. Or saying goodbye to the dog.

'You might have to get your own dog.'

'Maybe... One day, anyway.'

'Don't put it off. If you want something, go for it,' she said, thinking of her own new resolve.

Why shouldn't Zach have a dog? Yes, he worked long hours each day, but he could get a dog-sitter. Or put it into doggy daycare. Or bring it to work with him and train it to sleep in a corner whilst he saw patients? Well, maybe not the last thing. But he could find a way if he really wanted a dog of his own.

Lives were short. Time was short. You never knew when your life could change in an instant. You could get hit by a bus. Or have a roller coaster accident. And then you'd wish you'd taken the chance when you had it. Life was too short for regrets.

At the end of the walk she said goodbye to everyone and helped Elle and Dee load the borrowed dogs back into the van, until finally she was alone with Zach and Rebel.

'Want to join us for a last walk together?'

He had such a charming smile. Such a way with him that she couldn't resist. And honestly, she thought, why shouldn't she? She liked spending time with Zach, and Rebel was a lovely dog, and it was a beautiful day, and she didn't want to go back to Mrs Micklethwaite's yet. Her landlady was having her hall redecorated, and the workmen there had had their radios on and had been singing quite loudly when she'd left. She wasn't ready to go back to that noise.

'Why not?'

The village green was looking lovely. All the bunting was up now, and hanging baskets and lights had been strung up around lampposts and telegraph poles as the village prepared for the fete.

Zach let Rebel off the lead as they headed onto the green, and Hannah could see that in the duck pond today the small water fountain was working, sending up a spray of water in the centre. It was all very pretty.

Rebel went over to sniff at another dog—a small cockapoo that one of the locals was walking.

'The house is going to seem weirdly empty when he's gone,' said Zach.

'I bet.'

'I guess you never know what you've got until it's not there any more.'

Hannah nodded. She felt she knew that life lesson more than anyone.

'I've been thinking… About our practice dating.'

'Oh?' She turned to look at him briefly. Warily.

'I think we should stop,' he said.

'Oh. Okay…' It should be a relief. Why wasn't it a relief? Why was it disappointing?

He nodded. 'I think we both need to take the plunge. Stop practising and get real.'

She stared at him. What did he mean? With other people, surely? He didn't mean get real with each other? As in *each other*?

'Um…' She struggled to think of what to say. Not sure what she should say.

But Zach's gaze was pulled from her as the sound of splashing and barking came, and they both turned to see Rebel bounding through the water of the duck pond, sending ducks quacking and flapping in all directions, as he headed for the centre of the pond and the fountain!

'Oh, damn…' Zach ran over to the edge of the duckpond. 'Rebel! Rebel, come on, boy!'

Hannah smiled at first, then laughed as Rebel continued to utterly ignore everything Zach was saying. He was having tremendous fun, leaping about in the water, trying to catch the water droplets that shot from the fountain. The dog was having the time of his life.

'I think you might have to go in and get him.'

Zach turned to her, laughing. 'I'm not going in there.'

'It's just water.'

'Then you go in.'

'It's not my dog.' She smiled.

Zach grimaced and nodded. 'Rebel? Come on, boy! Biscuit! Look what I've got!'

He pretended to draw a biscuit from his pocket, but both he and Rebel knew that he was lying.

Rebel continued to leap about and play in the water. Zach sighed. 'Fine. Watch my shoes?'

Hannah laughed and nodded as Zach sat down to pull off his shoes, then his socks, and rolled up his jeans to his knees. He had nice legs...

He stood and let out a big sigh, staring at the playing dog for a moment, before he placed a foot in the water. 'Ooh, it's cold!' He pulled his foot out and turned to her, laughing.

Hannah smiled. 'Go on. Go and get him.'

'This isn't going to end well. I can feel it...' Zach took a tentative step into the cold pond water, grimacing as his toes touched the bottom. 'I don't know what's on the bottom of this pond, but I'm guessing it's not nice.'

She laughed. This was hilarious! His face was a picture, and her stomach hurt from laughing so much as he waded across the duck pond.

Other people stopped and stared, smiling and pointing, getting the attention of the people they were with and telling them to look at Zach as he waded through the water to an oblivious Rebel, who was still dancing and prancing and barking. Some people got out their phones. Began recording.

Zach wobbled, almost losing his balance. 'It's slippery!'

'You'll be fine!' she called, watching his progress as he got closer and closer to the happy, bouncing German Shepherd. Whatever happened, this dog was going to be exhausted after this walk!

Zach was getting close. He stopped. Obviously thinking about how to approach the dog. He unhooked the dog's lead from around his waist, where he'd clipped it to a belt loop, and took an unsteady step forward through the water.

But Rebel continued to bounce and splash and jump about, and when Zach stretched out to try and grab Rebel's collar the dog veered away, pulling at Zach, who was refusing to let go. Suddenly there was a yelp. A splash. A huge wave of water as Zach lost his footing and disappeared into the green murk.

Hannah burst into fresh laughter, bending double, as Zach burst to the surface, soaking wet and covered in algae and weeds and a brown silty substance that she didn't want to guess at.

He sat there in the middle of the duck pond and wiped his face free of water. And then he turned around and grabbed Rebel more securely this time and hooked on his lead.

Around the pond, everybody cheered—including Hannah—as a soaked Zach stood and took a bow and began to wade back through the water towards her. She had tears of laughter streaming down her face, and she'd also pulled her phone from her pocket and taken a picture of Zach emerging from the pond with Rebel like a rather more domestic-looking Poseidon.

'Are you okay?' she asked, still laughing, wiping away her happy tears with her sleeve.

'Bonny! Can't you tell?'

'You look like a swamp monster.'

He looked down at himself and laughed. 'Aye. I do a bit.'

'Let's get you back to your place. I'll get the dog cleaned up whilst you take a shower.'

Zach laughed and nodded.

CHAPTER ELEVEN

As soon as he got through the door of his house Zach began to strip off his clothes, pulling his shirt over the top of his head.

'What are you doing?' asked Hannah, looking slightly alarmed.

Oh. He'd been so desperate to get out of the damp, wet and dirty clothes, he'd not thought twice the second his front door had closed behind him.

But Hannah was trying not to look, and her cheeks were bright red, and he realised he must look a sight.

'Sorry. I'll take these off upstairs and grab a shower. If I leave them outside my bedroom door, would you be able to stick them in the machine for me?'

She nodded. 'And I'll put Rebel in the garden.'

'There's a hose out there. Could you wash him down?'

'Sure thing.'

She grabbed Rebel's lead and led him through the kitchen to the French doors, unlocked them and headed out.

Zach let out a breath and trotted upstairs, undoing his trouser button and zip as he went and stripping down to nothing once he got into the bathroom. He dropped the dirty clothes on to the landing area, and then turned on the shower and stepped under the lovely fresh and clean hot water spray.

It was a boon to his body, which had grown sticky and uncomfortable on the walk back from the duck pond. He had no doubt he was the talk of Greenbeck by now, and by Monday everyone would be talking about it at work.

Well, he could deal with that. He'd been the centre of gossip before. It passed. One day you were the hot topic...the next the village had moved on to bigger and better things. At least this time it was something funny.

The shower was making him feel much better, and he used plenty of shower gel to get rid of the 'Eau de Pond' smell he'd brought home with him. Shampoo. Conditioner. Body-wash. Within a few minutes, he felt clean, and he stepped out and wrapped a towel around his waist, ran his fingers through his hair.

He was just about to go to his room to pick

out some clean clothes, when he heard a shriek downstairs.

'Hannah? You okay?'

He heard a groan and, fearing she'd hurt herself, ran as fast as he could downstairs. He found her sitting on the kitchen floor.

He rushed to her side. 'What happened?'

She didn't answer. Not to begin with. She was staring at him, slightly open-mouthed. 'Erm... the floor was wet. I...um...slipped.'

Was she hurt?

She looked him up and down, seeming rather perturbed. 'You're wearing a towel,' she said.

He nodded. 'Aye.'

She swallowed hard and flushed. 'It's not much.'

'No, it's not.' He stared back at her, suddenly realising... Was she...*attracted* to him?

Hannah licked her lips and tore her gaze away, looking everywhere but at him. 'I should...um... go. Leave you to it. To get dressed. To...um...'

She glanced at him one last time and his gaze locked with hers.

'Hannah...?'

'Yes?' She was looking up at his face, her eyes wide and dark, her breathing rapid.

He felt the stirring of desire and knew that she was feeling the same. Had he been wrong about her feelings after all this time? He'd fought his for so long. His feelings for her. And now she was here. And he wasn't sure he could deny himself again.

'Please stay.'

She nodded.

And stepped forward into his arms.

When Zach had gone upstairs to get showered and changed Hannah had stood outside, hosing down the dog which had kept on trying to catch the water stream with his mouth. She had tried not to think of a naked Zach. She'd thought she'd been quite successful, too.

When the dog had been clean, and had shaken himself multiple times to shed the excess water trapped in his fur, she'd headed inside to the kitchen to find a towel to dry him with. Only instead, she'd slipped on the floor. Gone head over heels and landed on her bottom with a thump.

Pain had shot up her coccyx, so she'd not really heard Zach calling her name. And then suddenly he was there, running into the kitchen half-naked, clad only in the towel around his waist.

It had been quite a moment.

The pain in her coccyx had been forgotten.

The beauty of the man standing before her, pebbled with water droplets all over his wonderful muscles and dampening and darkening his chest hair, had been as if she was held in a mesmerising tractor beam, unable to tear her gaze away.

He'd held out his hand and pulled her to her feet, and that was when the delicious aromas had hit her nose. Whatever he'd showered with smelt divine. Sandalwood? Cedar with a hint of spice? Whatever it was, it was intoxicating!

He'd asked her a question, and she thought she'd answered, but she wasn't sure. She might even have said something obvious, about him only wearing a towel, and then her fight or flight instinct had kicked in and she'd known she ought to leave before she did something incredibly stupid. But then he'd asked her to stay, and there had been something in his eyes that melted her heart…

Now their fingers entwined as she stepped towards him. Hesitant. Uncertain. Doubtful. Because she could be misreading his attentions. Surely he couldn't want her? Could he?

But then he slipped a hand to the nape of her neck and pulled her close.

She closed her eyes and felt the soft warmth of his lips against hers. And her body woke up from the hibernation it had been in for far too long. A surge of electricity ignited all her nerve-endings and they waited, expectant, for his caress. No mere fireworks here—instead Hannah felt as if she was the birth of a new star. A supernova. She was blinded, stunned, shocked by how he made her feel, and all logical thought went out of the window as he pressed her back against the kitchen cabinets and ran his lips down the length of her throat.

She felt his hardness against her. She was lost. Overwhelmed. She'd fought this for so long, not believing for one minute that he had any interest in her, and now this… She couldn't fight it. Nor did she want to. Because she wanted him. Desperately!

She had tried to persuade herself that it could never happen, but now it was, and she really didn't want it to stop because it felt so unbelievably good. *He* felt good. Strong. Solid. She ran her hands down his back, came to the towel and pulled it open, dropping it to the floor and taking him in her hand.

She heard him draw in a shuddering breath. It was powerful. *She* had done this to him. *Her. Hannah.* She had turned him into this passionate, desirous man. He wanted her and she wanted him and nothing could stop them now. Reality? No. Sensibility? What was that?

She began to stroke him, and the growl in his throat was enough to send her over the edge. It felt as if she'd been waiting for this man for so long. Had been kept from him for far too long.

And yet at the same time she had been tempted and teased by him during those ridiculous fake dates they'd been having. So near and yet so far. He'd been a delicious temptation and now he was a delight she could savour—because all the pretence was gone now.

All the practice that they'd been hiding behind was out of the window. This was real. Very real. And she was going to savour every moment. Every kiss. Every touch. Every breath. Each moment was to be enjoyed to the full.,

His hands pulled her free of her top, his fingertips leaving a delicious trail over her skin, her shoulders, her back as he released her bra, gently and delicately removing the lace. And then her breast was in his mouth, and she realised she wanted his mouth elsewhere, too…

Could he read her mind? Because suddenly he got to his knees, kissing and licking a trail down over her stomach as he began to undo her trousers.

She felt an edge of panic, remembering her leg. Her prosthetic. But he'd seen it already—it wasn't as if it was a surprise. It wasn't going to put him off, was it?

Still she felt fear. Apprehension. Was it enough to make her call a stop to this?

No.

She wanted him. Far too much.

And when his lips pressed to her sex through the thin slip of her silken underwear her doubts fled. Disappearing like smoke. And then she was standing there, in his kitchen, in just her underwear, and he was kissing her *there*. With feather-light touches. Dampening the fabric with his hot mouth. Or maybe it was her own heat?

And then his fingers grasped the edge of the silk and slowly rolled it down, exposing her slowly. Kissing her. Licking her. Finding that sensitive spot and making her gasp out loud and clutch his hair…

She felt a vague awareness that they were in his kitchen, during daylight hours, with no curtains closed, but she couldn't remember if any houses overlooked Zach's back garden or not. She didn't think so. She thought they were safe. And one quick glimpse told her that the only being looking in on them was Rebel, who lay by the back door, panting from his exertions in the pond and looking at them quizzically.

A smile touched her lips as her head went back, and she breathed Zach's name as he pulled her trousers free from her legs. This was it. The moment in which he saw her leg not through being a doctor and her being his patient, but as a sexual partner. As someone he desired. Would it dull his response?

Clearly the answer was no, as he stood and

brought his mouth back to hers, hungry for her, hitching her up onto the kitchen counter, parting her legs and moving between them.

'Wait…we need a condom…' she said breathlessly, one hand on his chest.

'I don't think I have… Wait… There might be one upstairs. Hold on.'

And he scooped her up, held her around his waist and began to carry her up the stairs.

Hannah began to laugh. 'Seriously?'

'You bet,' he said, and he carried her as if she weighed no more than a feather up the stairs, across the landing and to his bedroom, where he gently lowered her onto his bed and reached across her to yank open the drawer of his bedside cabinet.

He rifled through books, papers, pens. Pulled out a few charging cables, tossing them to the floor, and then made a satisfied noise as his hand reached for a square packet that had been lurking right at the bottom.

'Aha!' He peered at it, turning it this way and that. 'Do these things have expiry dates?'

'Probably.'

'It's old.'

'How old?'

He grinned at her. 'Not so old. It's in date. Just!'

He showed her the expiry date. It expired in

one more month. Which made it okay. And then he used his teeth to tear the packet open and pull out the condom and she helped him put it on.

'Now, where were we? Oh, yes. I remember...' He grinned and kissed her again.

The bed was better than the kitchen counter. And when he finally entered her she clutched him to her and thought she would never let go.

To finally have Zach in her arms, wanting her, desiring her, was more than she could ever have hoped for.

Hannah woke much later, when the room was dark and quiet. Next to her, Zach was fast asleep, one arm flung over the top of his head, and for a brief moment she just watched him breathe.

He was a beautiful man, and what they'd shared had been beautiful. Truly. But now that her brain was no longer clouded by the joyous fog of oxytocin and endorphins, the reality of their situation began to encroach.

They had breached the barriers of friendship, work colleagues, boss and employee, and taken things to another level. They'd had sex. Seen each other. Tasted each other. Had laid each other bare, exposed themselves, and added a new, complicated dimension to their relationship.

They would have to face each other at work.

Pretend nothing had happened. Hide it from everyone else. Because she didn't want people knowing about this! It would be different if they were in a romantic relationship, but neither of them had set forth any demands of what they wanted from this.

What if it had just been lust?

What if he woke up and regretted it? Panicked? Had second thoughts like she was doing now?

The sex had been wonderful—of course it had. But it had placed them in jeopardy. If they both wanted more, then great. Maybe... But what would that mean? And when one of them wanted it to stop how awkward would that be?

They worked together! Would Hannah end up in the same situation as Stacey had once faced? Feeling ousted from a surgery she loved because people took sides? And although she thought she was liked, the village would take Zach's side, and living here in Greenbeck would become a miserable affair if the villagers took against her.

It all felt so uncertain, and yet her feelings for Zach ran so deep. The idea of losing him...

But she didn't want to outstay her welcome. Didn't want to...

Oh, my God, did we leave Rebel outside?

Hannah crept out of bed and grabbed a robe off the back of his bedroom door and slipped into it. She carefully opened the door—and almost fell as she tripped over a furry hazard.

Rebel got to his feet and looked at her curiously.

Zach must have woken up and let him in before going back to bed.

Crouching, she ruffled the dog's head. 'Hey, boy.' she whispered. 'Sorry about leaving you outside earlier.' She smiled. 'We were busy, huh?'

Rebel licked her cheek in response.

She smiled, then stood up. Her leg ached. She didn't usually sleep with her prosthetic on, but she must have drifted off after the sex. Lying in Zach's arms, she'd not wanted to leave them. They'd felt like the most perfect place to be.

So what to do now? Go back to his bed? Get a drink? She did feel thirsty…

Hannah tiptoed downstairs and found her clothes neatly folded on the back of a kitchen chair. Zach must have picked them up when he came down to see to the dog.

He was a good man. Maybe the best man.

And that scared the hell out of her.

If she went back up, what would that mean? She'd be signalling that she was happy. Content. Wanted more.

And she did want that.

But…

What if he didn't? What if last night had just been a fun interlude for Zach?

He didn't seem the type of guy who would be like that. He seemed genuine. But then she'd thought the same of Edward and she'd got that terribly wrong.

Could she trust her instincts this time?

As she dithered she heard noises upstairs. Unfamiliar creaks. Too late she realised that Zach was coming downstairs.

'Hannah?'

His voice came from the hall and she stood there, caught in the kitchen, holding her clothes to her chest.

He appeared in the doorway. Saw her holding her things. 'Are you *leaving*?'

'Um… I thought maybe I ought to. Before it gets light. I don't want people gossiping.'

'I don't care what other people say. Do you?'

'Yes. I know I shouldn't, but I do. Look, yesterday was great, but…'

He looked down at the floor, then up again. 'But?'

'I don't know if we made a mistake. Maybe we shouldn't have done what we did. Taken our relationship beyond being friends. We were just meant to be practising! Maybe we got caught up in the moment, like when we were skating, and maybe the feelings…none of them are real, and…'

Her voice trailed off as she saw the pain in his eyes, and briefly she wondered if *she'd* made a mistake. Had it been real for Zach? Did he want them to be together?

But then he ruined that illusion. 'Maybe you're right. If I've made you feel uncomfortable, I'm sorry. Perhaps we need some space from one another? We can do that—though I'd like to think we can be professional at work?'

His face was like stone. Blunt. Hard. Emotionless.

It broke her heart to know that she'd been right. It *had* been a mistake, and now everything was ruined and she had to get out of there!

'Of course. I need to get dressed…'

She pushed past him and headed into his living area and closed the door. She threw her clothes onto the couch and stripped off his robe as quickly as she could. The sooner she got out of here the better!

Tears pricked her eyes at the knowledge that she'd got it so horribly wrong with him, and that he had done a reverse turn just as quickly as she had. Now everything would be different, and by giving in to their desires and not thinking straight they had potentially ruined it all.

She sucked in a breath, wiped her eyes, picked

up his robe, folded it and placed it on the couch. Then she relaxed her shoulders and opened the door.

Zach was in the kitchen making coffee, as if nothing had happened, and it hurt that he could be so casual about this. So unaffected. It almost made her angry, and she wanted to beat her hands against his chest.

'I've left your robe on the couch,' she said.

'Uh-huh.' He sipped from his mug without looking at her.

'Give my best wishes to Marvin.'

He said nothing.

'I'll see you on Monday.'

And, with her heart breaking into millions of tiny pieces, she turned away from him, opened his front door and left.

When the front door had closed, Zach put his coffee mug down and propped himself against the counter, letting out a huge breath.

She'd said last night had been a mistake.

A mistake!

The fact that she thought the most beautiful thing he'd ever experienced in his entire life was a mistake astounded him! Shocked him to his core. How could she view what they'd done as something to regret and walk away from him when he had absolutely fallen hook, line and sinker for the woman? Had he been wrong? Again?

I thought I was right about her, but I was wrong. I'm so stupid!

Perhaps human beings were doomed to keep repeating the same mistakes they always made? Because it was hard-wired into their systems to learn from falling? They couldn't move forward without the scars to prove it.

But when do we have enough scars?

He'd thought she felt the same as him. That somewhere along the line their practice dating as friends had brought them closer and closer together. But yet again he'd been rejected. She knew he had a fear of rejection and yet she'd done this to him! It was cruel. It was...

He sighed and banged a fist down on the counter, making Rebel flinch.

'Sorry, boy.' He crouched down and Rebel came to him. Sat beside him and licked his leg. 'I've got to say goodbye to you today, too, haven't I?'

When Marvin came home he'd lose Rebel, too. No Hannah. No Rebel. No close friend. And awkwardness at work, no doubt.

He leaned back against the kitchen cabinets and watched the clock until it was time to fetch Marvin from the hospital.

CHAPTER TWELVE

HANNAH ALMOST CALLED in sick on Monday morning. But she knew she couldn't let down all those people who were booked in for appointments and so she went in early. Head down. Staying in her room. Taking in enough food and drinks so that she didn't have to venture into the staffroom with everyone else.

With Zach.

A knock at her door on at lunchtime scared her to death. What if it was Zach? But it wasn't. It was Stacey—Dr Emery.

'Just checking to see if you're okay? I haven't seen you all morning.'

'I'm fine!' she said brightly, relieved that it was her and not a tall, brooding, rejected Dr Zachary Fletcher.

'You sure?'

'Absolutely! Just catching up on some admin and a few referrals from last week.'

'Okay. Well, if you need anything…'

'Thanks.'

She let out a huge sigh when Stacey left.

As the days passed, she kept hearing Zach's deep voice through the walls, from his consulting room next to hers. Occasionally she heard him laugh out loud, and realised that he was absolutely fine with what had happened! She almost wanted to storm next door and rant and rave at him, ask him why he was so unaffected. Wasn't he supposed to be afraid of being rejected? Like her?

It was eating her alive!

She wasn't sleeping. Wasn't eating.

But worst of all she missed him so much!

Zach had become her everything. Not just a great boss and colleague, but an amazing friend and someone she enjoyed spending time with.

One morning, when it had become very hot in her room, she stepped outside for some fresh air, standing where Zach had used to keep Rebel. Seeing the empty space where the dog had been almost broke her heart. Her bottom lip began to tremble and quiver, and it took a huge amount of energy to force the tears away.

Everything had changed, and people were starting to ask questions. They'd noticed a difference in her. They were being respectful and keeping their distance, not being too pushy, but she could see that people cared. Which was nice.

Although the one person she wanted to talk to the most, she couldn't.

There'd been an awkward moment that morning, when one of Zach's patients had come to see her about some headaches she'd been having. When Hannah had performed a blood pressure check, she had discovered her BP was through the roof. Dangerous levels. She'd had to knock on his door and ask him what he wanted her to do. Usually with a high blood pressure they'd send a patient home with a monitor to check their BP twice a day, every day for a week, but this patient's readings were so high Hannah had been worried about the stroke risk.

And Zach's face on seeing her appear in his room... He'd looked shocked, then uncomfortable, and then he'd been businesslike. Abrupt.

It had hurt.

She couldn't be like this with him. She wanted them to go back to the way they'd been before. Carefree. Happy. Joyful. Spending time together. Seeing him smile and knowing that she'd caused it. Going for a walk and hearing him laugh at some silly thing. Holding his hand. Being in his arms again...

I love him.

The realisation was startling. But she'd known the truth of it, deep down, for some time. She'd just been ignoring it. Pretending it wasn't really happening. Because if it was, then it was putting her heart in jeopardy. It was a hopeless love. A fatal love. It couldn't live. He didn't want her. Not the way she wanted to be wanted. Fearlessly. Hopelessly. Eternally. Unconditionally.

And if I love him, and can't have him, how do I get through my days?

It was the morning of the village fete. The sun was shining, the sky was blue, birds were singing and the bunting was dancing in the breeze. Children were smiling...families looked happy. He should be feeling joyful, but Zach was feeling anything but.

He felt lost. Unmoored. Alone. He was surrounded by friends and people who liked him, but it didn't seem to matter a jot without Hannah being there.

How had it all gone so wrong? He'd thought, when they'd finally given in to their desires and slept with one another, that their path would be smooth. There would be no hiding any more, they'd each shown that they wanted the other, so surely it ought to be plain sailing from there?

But no. He'd caught her trying to creep out of his house. Without a goodbye. And she'd looked regretful. Said that they'd made a mistake. He'd realised suddenly, startlingly, that he was being left behind again. Not good enough.

It had hurt so much, like being stabbed in the heart, that he'd immediately gone on the defensive. His walls had gone up, he'd gone quiet, as he always did, and then later, he'd collected Marvin from hospital.

Even Marvin had asked him if everything was all right. Said that he seemed different. And then he'd had to say goodbye to the dog.

He was only next door. Zach could hear him in Marvin's garden. But he missed him. Rebel had been his companion as his relationship with Hannah had developed. Or he thought it had developed...

Wasn't he supposed to have learned from his past? Wasn't he supposed to have learned from his mistakes in trusting that a woman he desired felt the same way as him?

He'd been so sure she felt the same way that night! Being with her physically, he'd felt they were equals, that they were both there because it was what they wanted. So much!

This past week had been a torment. She'd been avoiding him. People at work had noticed she was staying in her room and asked him if he knew what was going on, if anything? He'd had to shrug. To pretend he didn't know. He'd told them to give her time, that maybe she just needed some space. When all he'd really wanted to do was go to her, wrap his arms around her, and whisper into her hair that everything was going to be all right.

Only he couldn't, and that was tearing him in two.

And now he had to judge a babies' fancy dress competition. With Stacey and Daniel. He had to go to the fete and paste on a smile and pretend that everything was hunky-dory in his life. When it wasn't. When what he wanted was to find Hannah. Tell her that… Tell her…

Tell her I love her? And make her run away some more?

She'd probably leave the surgery. Leave Greenbeck. And that was the last thing he wanted to happen. He needed her in his life, and if it was to just be his friend, then that would have to do. Even if it meant seeing her with someone else.

No, that's not true. I don't think I could bear that. So, should I tell her?

Although saying *I love you* to Hannah seemed fatalistic to him, she thought they'd made a mistake. Telling her would just make her think that he couldn't let go and refused to be abandoned again. Wouldn't it?

But what if she was just as afraid as him? He knew she could be, because she'd been abandoned, too. Maybe her reaction that morning was because reality had set in and she hadn't seen a way forward? What if she needed *him* to declare how serious he was about *her*? She'd been humiliated in love before. Had thought her ex was putting just as much as she was into the relationship. And she'd been wrong. What if she was just scared?

She'd stood in front of a mirror wearing a wedding dress, getting ready to show the world that she wanted to marry her man, and he had made a fool of her. Jilted her on their wedding day via a cowardly text message. *A text message!*

Maybe she would be afraid of what she felt for him until she knew for sure what he felt for her was just as strong?

His mind began to race. Going backwards and forwards on *what ifs* and *maybes*.

If he could somehow show her what she meant to him. Tell her. Let the whole world know that he loved her and that he would put himself out there for her, no matter the risk to him…

Would that be enough?

Would that win him the girl?

His love?

Because if she loved him, too—and he hoped that she did—then she would make him the happiest man on the planet.

The question was…was he brave enough to risk it?

CHAPTER THIRTEEN

HER INSTINCT HAD been not to go to the Green-beck village fete. Zach would be there. He'd been asked to judge a babies' fancy dress competition, so he would definitely be there. And she missed seeing him. Missed just being near him. And because there would be plenty of crowds she thought she'd be able to lose herself in them and he wouldn't notice her watching him.

I just want to make sure he's okay.

He probably was.

People seemed to have no problem in walking away from her.

But her heart ached for him so she decided to go. It would be better than staying in the house. Mrs Micklethwaite was out for the day, and she didn't want to sit at home alone. Was it better to be lonely surrounded by other people? Probably.

She cycled there, propping up her bike by a lamppost and locking it, knowing it would still be there on her return. She didn't plan on staying long. Just long enough to reassure herself that he was okay.

The fete seemed to be in full swing when she got there. Full of marquees, and people milling around, the air filled with the scent of candy floss and burgers and coffee.

As she passed the refreshments tent she felt a hand upon her arm.

'Nurse?'

'Mr Fisher! Hello, how are you?' Jerry Fisher was the gentleman who had joined her dog-walking group after coming to see her with imagined ailments because he'd been so lonely. He was standing next to another gentleman, who was holding on to the lead of a dog she recognised.

'Rebel?'

'This is Marvin. He's just come out of hospital,' said Jerry, introducing them.

Zach's neighbour. 'Of course. How are you, Marvin?'

'Much better now I'm out of that place. All you doctors and nurses do a wonderful job, but there's nothing quite like being at home, is there?' He smiled, patting the dog's head. 'You know Rebel?'

'I got to know him when Dr Fletcher was

minding him for you. They came on our group's walks once or twice.'

Marvin nodded and smiled. 'Oh, there he is! Dr Fletcher!'

Hannah froze, her heart thudding in her chest.

'Oh, I don't think he heard me,' said Marvin, shrugging. 'I'll get a hold of him later, no doubt.'

Hannah let out a tense breath. 'I must be off. Nice seeing you both.'

She smiled and slipped away from the tent, glancing in both directions to see which way Zach had gone. It was hard to see, because there were so many people, but she thought she could see him up ahead. He was quite tall, compared to most people. Logic told her to walk in the other direction, but her heart propelled her after him. She tried to tell herself that she would keep her distance. But the need to be near him was overpowering.

A group of people emerged from the beer tent and she lost sight of him. She struggled to make her way through the crowd, to keep track of him, but he was lost.

As the crowd thinned out, Hannah let out a short, frustrated breath.

'Hannah?'

She turned. 'Zach…'

He was there. Right there. Standing before her, looking as handsome as ever, and she knew in that moment that her heart was hopelessly lost to him and always would be.

'I thought it was you,' he said. 'How are you?'

She swallowed. How to answer? Lie and tell him she was fine? Or tell him the truth? Tell him that she *had* made a mistake. A mistake in thinking that the right thing to do was walk away from him because she was afraid.

'I've been... I don't know how I've been. Confused, mainly.'

He nodded.

Behind them one of the organisers, Walter, was up on a dais with his megaphone, asking all competitors for the babies' fancy dress competition to make sure they were at the main tent for one o'clock.

Zach stared at her. It was too loud for him to speak. Then, when the noise lessened, he said, 'I've missed you.'

Her heart skipped a beat. 'Me too.'

He looked at her then. And his eyes were filled with hope.

'What happened between us was not a mistake, Hannah. Nothing that amazing could be a mistake. What we did afterwards? Absolutely— for sure. But *before*? Being with you...getting to know you...enjoying spending time with you... All of that was perfect. All of that was *meant to be*.'

Her heart filled with joy at his words.

Zach stepped closer to her. One step. Two. And then he reached for her hands, entwining his fingers around hers.

'I'm sorry if I ever made you feel like you weren't enough. I never meant to. Because you *are* enough. You are more than that. *Enough* doesn't sound like a big enough word for what you mean to me, so I want to show you. I want to prove to the world what you mean to me— what you will always mean to me.'

Hannah was beaming, happy tears in her eyes, and she nodded, speechless.

Zach smiled, and turned to take hold of Walter's megaphone as he stepped down from his dais. 'Can I just borrow this for a moment, please, Walter?'

He stepped on to the dais.

What was he going to do?

Hannah squeezed his hand and stood beside him on the platform, suddenly nervous.

'Can I have everyone's attention, please?' said Zach.

She almost froze as everyone turned to listen to him. All eyes were on them.

Zach was smiling. He had the look of a man who was determined to do something, no matter what, and knew that the adrenaline of the moment would carry him through.

'My name is Dr Zachary Fletcher. Most of you know me. I work at the Greenbeck village surgery and this lovely woman to my left…' he turned to smile and wink at Hannah '…is our advanced nurse practitioner, Hannah Gladstone. She is not only a stunning nurse but a wonderful human being, and I want you all to know…' He paused, turned to her. Looked her directly in the eyes. 'That I love her with all my heart.'

She stared at him. The villagers forgotten. The fete forgotten. All she saw was him. All she heard…all she felt…were his words and their meaning.

He loved her.

He loved her!

'I love you, too,' she said, and everyone around them began to clap.

She took a step towards him, threw her arms around his neck and kissed him—right there and then on the stage.

His arms went around her, his eyes sparkled with happiness and delight, and she kissed him again and again.

'I knew I was right about you,' he said.

She smiled. 'How do you mean?'

'From that very first day we met. You told me you were absolutely tip-top.'

And Hannah smiled and laughed and kissed him again.

EPILOGUE

HANNAH STOOD IN her wedding dress in front of the mirror, smiling at her phone and the latest text from Zach.

I love you. I can't wait to marry you. See you at the end of the aisle!

He'd sent so many texts. There'd even been a video message from him. A compilation of shots of him getting dressed for their wedding. His clothes laid out on the bed. The pink rose for his buttonhole. Zach wearing just a white shirt, boxer shorts and dark socks, with Daniel helping him do his tie. The next was him buttoning his trousers. Shrugging on his jacket. Fastening the cufflinks. Checking he had her wedding ring with a big smile on his face. All set to music she loved.

She had no fear today.

This wedding day was the one she'd been

practising for. Her real wedding day. The one she'd been meant to have.

But Zach knew how scary this day would be for her. How she might have flashbacks to the last time she'd stood in a wedding gown. And he was doing everything in his power to make her know that he would be there at the end of the aisle.

She did not doubt him.

She had no second thoughts.

No cold feet.

Because her love for him was absolute and it knew no bounds. Everyone said they were perfect together and she knew they were right.

Stacey, her maid of honour, was dressed in a soft pink gown and came up to her to fiddle with her veil. 'Are you ready?' she asked.

Hannah nodded. 'I am.'

Another text beeped into her phone.

Don't be too late. I've already waited far too long in my life to find you. I love you.

Smiling, she typed her reply, and once she'd pressed 'send', Stacey took her phone from her.

'That's enough. You're going to see him in a few minutes and then you can spend the rest of your lives showing each other how much you love each other.'

'I can't believe I'm about to marry him.'

'No? I don't see why. We could all tell it was going to happen.'

'Really?'

Stacey nodded. 'Now, come on. I need this ceremony to be on time. Baby Esme will need a feed in exactly sixty minutes.'

Esme was the beautiful baby girl that Stacey and Daniel had had together. Another workplace romance... The people in the village had begun calling the surgery Cupid's Bow, which made them smile.

They'd all come to Greenbeck to find something. They hadn't known what it was, but here they had found their true love. Their happiness. One another.

The sleek grey car didn't have far to go to take Hannah and her father to the church. She knew half the village was going to be there, and could feel butterflies dancing in her stomach.

Alighting from the car, she posed for the photographer a few times, then Stacey handed over her bouquet of pink roses and she began to walk up the small curving path towards her destiny.

Inside, the organ began to play 'The Wedding March' and she heard the scuffle of many people getting to their feet. She looked at her father.

'Okay?' he asked.

'I'm more than okay.'

They stepped forward into the church and all eyes turned to her.

Hannah blushed at the attention, but then she set her eyes on Zach at the end of the aisle and he turned to see her, his face breaking out into the broadest smile she had ever seen, and that was all she needed to see. All she was aware of after that.

Her husband-to-be.

Dr Zachary Fletcher.

And at his feet their adopted dog, Bonnie. A black Labrador who had stolen their hearts from the moment they'd first seen her at the shelter. She had a pink bow tied around her neck to match the buttonholes.

Zach looked so handsome, and she saw him wipe away a tear of happiness as she walked towards him.

When she got level with him, he leaned in. 'You look beautiful. I'm so lucky.'

She beamed. 'So am I. The luckiest girl in the world.'

She wanted to lean in and kiss him. Kiss him now. But there would be a time and a place for that in this ceremony. Her next kiss with Zach would be as his proud, happy, and eternally in love *wife*.

They turned to face the vicar, hand in hand. Dog at their feet. Tail wagging. And they began to say their vows.

* * * * *

If you missed the previous story in the Greenbeck Village GP's duet, then check out

The Brooding Doc and the Single Mom

If you enjoyed this story, check out these other great reads from Louisa Heaton:

Miracle Twins for the Midwife
A Date with Her Best Friend
Their Marriage Worth Fighting For

All available now!